Devils & Pretty Sins
Book 1

UNDER HIS COMMAND

RHEA HARP

Devils & Pretty Sins Book 1

UNDER HIS COMMAND

RHEA HARP

To the girls who love being teased and edged, remember...
Don't you dare come until he commands you.

PUBLISHER'S NOTE

Under His Command is a work of fiction and does not fully adhere to traditional military ranks or structures. The story is intended for entertainment purposes. So I've taken creative liberties to turn this into the most gripping story I knew I could write.

If you are looking for complete accuracy to real-life military practices, stop reading here–this book is probably not going to be your jam. But if you *are* curious to step into my world, feel free to turn that page. Commander Rowan King will be taking very good care of you.

Lastly, please remember this is a dark romance. A lot of my writing contains mature themes. Content tags are located on my website (rheaharp.com) which lists out the themes, tropes, and topics for this story. Your mental health matters, so please be sure to check those before reading the book.

ONE

Five years ago

I blink once, and the smoke is everywhere. In the car, surrounding the car—everywhere. I cough into my elbow, stabbing the seat belt buckle with my other hand until it sets me free. I stumble into the street, tears burning the backs of my eyes both from the dark cloud of chemicals, and from the frustration coursing through me.

It's the second time it's happened this month, even though I've already spent all my savings on the repairs. They told me there was a problem with the brakes, but Trent insisted they were morons and asked them to check the coolant system instead. In the end, neither the mechanics nor my ex-boyfriend figured out what the hell was wrong with my brother's old Honda.

They still took my money—*a shit move on their part*—and now I'm left with a smoking car in the middle of the road, just a few feet away from my parents' house. *Great.*

Pulling my T-shirt over my nose, I open the hood and look at the engine as if I know how to fix this myself. I start touching random parts until I stain my fingers with oil and dirt, making me curse out loud.

But I don't curse the car. Or my brother. Instead, I curse my dad, who should have taught me how to handle shit like this before he ran off with his mistress, leaving his family behind. Even if I wanted to call him for help, he wouldn't answer. He hasn't—not since he left, anyway.

And my brother... I'd call Cole in a heartbeat if he wasn't fighting for his life in the war zone of the Sylvestrian Ridge. So I pull the hood of his Honda back down and accept the fact that I'll have to take a few extra shifts at the cafe to get the car towed into the repair shop. *Again.*

After locking the doors, I peer through the thick cloud of smoke when the figure of a man standing in front of my parents' house enters my visual field. He's tall and built like an armored wall—taut muscles rippling through the tailored army uniform as he extends his hand forward to knock on the door of our house.

I keep my distance, but go around him to see a glimpse of his face. The sun moves behind his profile as I turn, casting a golden glow on the sharp structure of his jaw and making it appear even more prominent. The other side of his face, the one dipped in shadow, shows me the color of his eyes. They gleam like polished malachite, a green so chaotic, so uneven that almost sends a shiver down my spine.

He knocks on the door one more time, and the sound opens up the vault of anxiety deep within me. Instantly my heart drops, a pit forms low in my stomach, and my palms break out in a sweat all at the same time. Why would the army be here, on a Tuesday morning, when my brother isn't scheduled to come home for another three months?

Why else, Dove? Because he's dead. Because your nightmares were real.

A thick web of unshed tears pools around my eyes, but I blink them away, refusing to bring the thought to life. Cole isn't dead. He can't be, because he promised he'd come home in time for my high school graduation. He promised he'd take me to the beach with his friends this summer before I head off to college.

He never did keep his promises though, did he?

I don't realize I'm standing dangerously close to the man until after he turns around to meet my eyes. And when he does, a wave of raw, primal energy rolls off of him, coiling around my body like a tempestuous flame. I can feel it squeezing my lungs, trapping all the air inside me and making my cheeks flush.

He cocks his head to the right, observing me, his eyes darkening to the color of the leaves in the shadows. The summer breeze dances through his naturally tousled, velvet-black hair, causing a few rebel strands to sway across his eyes like phantoms.

For some reason, the way he looks at me makes me feel exposed—naked almost, even though his gaze hasn't left mine long enough to take in the rest of my petite body. Still, I wrap my arms around myself, my breathing shallow as I try to think of something to say. Anything.

"Dove Finnegan?"

The way my name rolls off his tongue finally draws the trapped air in my lungs out.

"T-that's me," I stutter.

For a second, his somber face seems to soften, a sad and kind half-smile stretching across his lush lips. I can tell it's not meant to be seductive, but goddamn, he looks good doing that. I want him to do it again–

No. Get a hold of yourself, Dove. What the hell.

"Are your parents around?"

I shouldn't tell him the truth. Is he really from the army? He could be anyone. With a smile and a face like that, he could be anybody. I steal a glance at the military medals adorning his broad, muscular chest. Since when do they put men so young and handsome into leadership positions? He looks to be about the same age as my brother—in his late twenties.

"My mother is at work. And my father moved out."

I'm not even sure why I mentioned my father. I tend to avoid thinking about him or bringing him up. But for some reason, it feels like if this man asks anything of me, my mind and body will give him what he wants.

"Okay," he says, offering a soft nod—too soft to suit him and his ascetic figure. I'm almost angry at the gentleness of it. "Here's what you're going to do, then, Dove. You're going to go inside, bring me a glass of water, and then sit on the stairs in front of your house while you listen to what I have to say. Do you understand?"

His voice is grave now, intimidating, as if I'm one of his soldiers... or a little sister he has to keep out of trouble for his mother's sake. I gulp once, nodding, and struggle to grasp the odd sensation taking over me.

"Good girl."

My cheeks flush and heat flares low in my stomach as the words leave his mouth, taking me by surprise. Our eyes lock. His eyebrows lift ever so slightly as he takes a sharp breath in, and I can just tell that there's something there, in the depths of his gaze, that's now mixing with mine.

Time stops for a moment, only resuming when he drags a hand down his face and breaks contact. He steps back into the street to let me get into my house, and I remember the command he issued me. He walks past me, the smell of leather and pine and something muted, like amber, enters my nostrils with ease, hugging every nerve ending I have and making sure I'll remember it for the rest of my life. I go inside, and with trembling hands I run water from the tap into a tall glass, bringing it back outside as carefully as I can in my disoriented state.

"Did you want the water?"

He shakes his head, and I sit down on the porch at the same time, as instructed.

"The water is for you."

And then I understand why he issued his command.

His lips start moving, but the low, dark voice fades out as I go deeper and deeper into myself, the world around me becoming a blur. A blur where all I hear are words like "Cole Finnegan was a good man," and "I'm sorry, Dove," and "he fought well," and other things I wish I could just block out of my mind.

The tragic news shreds my heart open right in front of this man, leaving me raw and vulnerable under his gaze. I look up at him through wet eyelashes, and the tears won't stop coming, no matter how much I try to hold them back. My head feels light, and my limbs so heavy. I feel completely disoriented. Flashes of my last memories with Cole race through my mind, coming to a sudden halt at that damned morning he left for the army, a few years ago.

"Just go," I tell him, sniffing as I clutch my pillow at my chest. "Leave, if that's what you want. I don't care." I keep my gaze focused on the window, away from him. The weight of his body is pressed down into the couch. I expect him to just sigh and give up comforting me, but he doesn't. He takes his time.

"It's not forever. I'll be back before you know it," he says, his voice soft and understanding. I hate this. I hate that he's still looking at me like I'm just a kid. Because I'm not. I simply don't want him to go out there and lose his life. He says it's for me and Mom, but we never asked for that.

"When? When exactly will you be back?" I ask. He keeps silent, the answer clear enough. I shake my head, a bittersweet smile spreading on my lips as I let out a sharp exhale.

His strong arms wrap around my torso, pulling me closer to him. I want to show him I'm mad, but I end up giving in to the hug. This might be our last moment together for God knows how long. He holds me tight at his chest, his chin resting on top of my head as he says, "I'll be back. I swear it. You just wait and see."

The man crouches down in front of me, his thumb brushing a tear from my cheek. It brings me back to the present moment. The touch is soft, almost reverent, and a shudder runs through me—not from desire, but from the sudden intensity of the moment. His hand lingers, warm and calloused, grounding me in a way I didn't expect.

"I know," he murmurs, his voice a low rasp that cuts through the haze of my grief. "Cole was like a brother to me. So I know, Dove."

His words should comfort me, and maybe they do in some way, but the weight of my loss presses down hard. The simple act of his thumb brushing my cheek draws more tears, and I lean into him without thinking. The steady beat of his heart against my cheek is a strange reprieve. It reminds me of Cole—of the countless times he comforted me just like this. Only the things I used to cry about back then were nothing more than fleeting teenage dramas.

For a moment, I forget everything. The pain, the smoke, the world around us—it all fades. There's only his presence, his strength. And that makes something else stir inside me, something I'm not ready to feel. Not now. Instead, more memories of my brother flood my mind like a river breaking its banks.

"Hey, kid," my brother says into the phone after I pick up. His voice is playful, but not like it once was. A testament to the harsh conditions and tormenting days spent between bullets, screams, and the corpses of both his

enemies and brothers-in-arms.

"Cole!" I smile, silently waving goodbye to my small group of girlfriends in front of our local high school. "What's going on–? Don't tell me! Are they sending you home?"

A laugh. "You have to stop asking me that, or I'll never get the chance to surprise you like you see in those videos online."

I roll my eyes, even though I know he can't see it. "I don't want to be surprised. I just want to know."

"Well, how's this for a surprise?" he says, and my pulse rises in anticipation. "This summer. You, me, and some of my friends. We're going out to Myrtle Beach for a week. You can even bring that crazy Chelsea girl from school if you want."

My lips part, and all my face muscles go taut with a broad smile. "Are you serious?! Oh, my God, I'm so, so excited!" I hear him chuckle on the other line, but then I frown, remembering how strict Mom can be. "But wait, what if mom won't let me–"

"Already talked to her. You're coming, and we'll take care of you. All you have to do is say yes."

I go home that afternoon with my heart full of hope and my mind buzzing with enthusiasm. My brother is coming home. And I get to spend a whole week with him without a care in the world.

The man in front of me swipes his thumb across my face one last time, and I snap back to reality. To the present. To the world without my brother. Cole is truly gone, and loneliness starts making its nest deep into the hollow of my heart. That's why there's a hum beneath my skin—something low, something confusing. The man's touch is a lifeline, but there's an undercurrent of something deeper, something I don't want to acknowledge.

"What's your name... sir?" I whisper, my voice shaking as I try to focus on anything but the gaping hole in my chest.

His eyes flicker, his nostrils flaring ever so slightly. "Rowan King," he says, and his name rolls off his tongue with an authority that makes my stomach clench.

He suddenly stands, his towering frame casting a shadow over me, and instinctively I reach for his hand. He pulls me to my feet, and I stumble forward, colliding into his chest. Everything stops. I'm wrapped in his arms, held tightly against him, and it feels... safe. Safe in a way that makes the grief feel distant, if only temporarily.

But the safety comes with a cost. The feel of his hard chest, the heat radiating from his body—it sparks something I don't want to admit is there. I feel Rowan's hands tighten around me, his fingers brushing the small of my back. My breath hitches, and guilt floods me. How can I feel this now? How can I want to be closer to him, when all I should feel is loss?

"Rowan," I whisper, my voice cracking. I shouldn't say it. I shouldn't even think it. But I feel weak, and the pain keeps crushing my soul, and I want to cling on to something else for just a second. So I end up saying it anyway. "It's okay if you want to kiss me."

The words leave my mouth before I can stop them,

and a wave of shame crashes over me. I feel pathetic, confused, and so desperately alone. What am I asking for? I don't even know anymore.

His grip tightens. For a moment, I think he might give in. His gaze falls to my lips, and I can see the same conflict in his eyes. But then, with a slow exhale, he pulls back.

"I can't let that happen, Dove. Not today, at least." A short pause, and then–"You're grieving. It wouldn't be right."

His words are firm, but there's a softness to them too, and that softness brings fresh tears to my eyes. He presses his lips to my forehead—a chaste kiss, but one that makes me feel like I'm crumbling inside. It's too much and not enough all at once.

"Take care of yourself, Dove Finnegan," he says, slowly drifting away from me.

His body leaves mine, my hair falls back on my shoulders, and I have no choice but to watch him walk back to a black SUV parked a few houses down the street. I wrap my arms around myself, the grief he temporarily took away from me now hitting me like a tsunami wave.

I look back at the glass of water sitting on the porch and then I break, letting it all come out of me until my throat feels raw and my bones ache from the weight of my brother's death.

TWO

Three years later

The sound of billiard balls hitting the table's corners mixed with the stench of cheap beer fill the air. My best friend, Sterling, is here. Her boyfriend too, and the date they insisted I said yes to so I could stop feeling like I'm third-wheeling all the time.

I can feel Jared's hand resting on my naked knee, caressing it in circles with his thumb while he talks about entanglement, and quantum mechanics, and everything I don't give a crap about.

This isn't even why I didn't want to go out with him. Because on the rare occasions when he's not monopolizing the conversation with his physics-related topics, he's actually an okay guy. He's tall, and flirty, and has that air about him that says, "I'm the bad guy your mom doesn't want you around."

Strange combination, I know.

And maybe I *would've* been interested in him, with my daddy issues and all, if there wasn't another man already haunting my dreams every night.

A man I've never had, nor that I'll ever have. A man that sparked something in me that day, when he pulled my hair, tasted my tears, and called me his good girl.

I tried forgetting about him—because there was no point in hanging onto a fantasy. There still isn't. But every time his name pops up in the news or on the TV, my pussy clenches and I get that vibrant flush in my cheeks Sterling always teases me about.

I couldn't push this man out of my memory ever since that day. As I grieved the death of my brother, the thought of Rowan King seemed to tamp down my suffering. The more I thought about him, the more I remembered—Cole had actually told me about his two best friends in the army.

He told me about Rowan and the other man in their small group, but he never called them by name. That summer, before he died, we were supposed to meet. Cole promised he was going to take me with them on a trip to the beach. It would've been my first unsupervised vacation. A sad smile stretches across my lips as I remember how excited I was at the thought of hanging out with them.

"Oh my God!" Sterling suddenly shrieks. "Look, Dove, it's your sexy-ass commander on TV! Hey, Bree," she shouts over to the girl at the bar, "turn that shit up, will you? God, he really is hot." She wiggles her eyebrows at me.

I can only giggle in response to show her it's nothing but a stupid crush, but I know the truth. I can feel the need slowly building up in my core, tingling at the entrance of my pussy. Expecting him. Opening up for him. It's dangerous and wrong, but I can't help it. I can't help but want him with every fiber of my being.

"You can't be saying other guys are hot. You're taken!" Sterling's boyfriend, Lucian, protests.

"He's not just a guy, Luce dear. He's Commander of the Army. And he's most definitely a *man*, not a *guy*."

Lucian scoffs, and pushes her head down toward his crotch making some joke about how he's *all man*. We all know what he's referring to, and Jared laughs beside me, reminding me that he's here. But all my attention is now on Rowan—who's looking more handsome than ever here on the wall of this filthy bar in the university campus.

"...the attack on the small southwestern town in the Sylvestrian Ridge killed more than one hundred and twenty people tonight. I have Commander Rowan King joining me live tonight. Commander, this was a difficult operation for you and your team, no doubt. Did you see this attack coming?"

I lean back in my chair, catching a better glimpse of that velvet-black hair and those calculated eyes, but it's his voice that has me in shambles.

Good girl.

You're grieving. It isn't right.

Take care of yourself, Dove Finnegan.

"Yes," Rowan answers, his tone low and grave, and completely sure of himself. "Our intelligence did see this coming, since the CCSI has already attacked the northwestern villages. We were able to keep the situation under control and push back the coalition. But unfortunately, lives were still lost tonight."

The news station host, Van Reynolds, starts grilling him for details. I hate the guy. He built his entire career on eliciting dramatic reactions out of the most influential people in the country.

And now that the chain of command has been unified from multiple Combatant Commanders to just one... Rowan has been in the spotlight for quite some time. Judging by the way he's shooting arrows through his eyes at Van, I'd say he isn't a big fan of all this unwanted attention.

And, I mean, I know his methods for pushing back this war are rather... unconventional. Rumor has it the cyber-attack on the CCSI, our current enemy, was his doing. That the two preemptive strikes were nothing but an ego-boosting measure for Rowan. And I've even heard proxy forces were used six months ago for targeted assassinations.

But even if Rowan *did* deploy all these orders, the CCSI fucking deserves it.

They've killed civilians. Children, too. Pushed the villagers living in the Ridge into a corner, breaking families apart and causing immense suffering. And for what? A bunch of gold in the remaining mines in the area?

I shake my head. The news station shows a few more videos of Rowan getting out of a helicopter, then walking alongside the lieutenant colonels and majors under his command.

Van Reynolds keeps talking, but I'm forcing myself

to stop paying attention, since I don't want Sterling to make fun of my stupid little crush even more.

"...it's not like she doesn't want to, right, Dove?" Sterling asks.

"Huh?"

"Jared was just saying how he wants to pick you up for the picnic this weekend. That's sweet, right?"

I turn my head toward him, a smirk already plastered on his face.

"I told you, I need to secure an internship by the end of the semester. I was counting on writing some more applications this weekend."

"Oh, come now," Jared smiles. "It'll be fun."

"So will securing a job at a law firm after graduation." I slurp the last drops of my Coke through the straw.

Sterling rolls her eyes dramatically. "Everyone knows you're going to get one. Live a little—you've got plenty of time to stick your nose up in boring case files next year."

"I'm sorry," I say, an apologetic smile spreading across my face.

Sterling narrows her eyes at me, a silent message indicating that we're not done talking about this.

That night, I go home alone and spread my pussy open, imagining that Rowan is watching me, praising me, and using me in all the ways only he knows how to do.

I fall asleep excited to dream of him again, but in the morning, I realize the dream never came.

That was the first night I hadn't dreamed about

Rowan.

THREE

Present Day

I'm filing away my boss's backup documents for court on Monday when my phone rings, an unknown number flashing on the screen. I groan, my head throbbing from yet another sleepless night being Miss Pratt's second brain.

It's not easy training under a world-class lawyer, but I didn't expect it to be. Just the fact that I've managed to secure my position here after winning my internship at her law firm three years ago should be a celebration in itself. And most days, it is. Most days, when the loneliness doesn't overtake me like it did today.

I pick my phone up from the desk, placing down the papers cradled at my chest. It's 7 p.m., and I haven't made plans with anyone. Not since Lucian and Sterling—my only friends—are still busy fucking on their honeymoon in Bali.

Reluctantly, I accept the call and put the phone to my ear, only to be met with silence from the other end of the line. I frown, looking at the screen to see if we're still connected. We are.

"Hello? Who is this?"

Shuffling and breathing, but still no words.

I curse under my breath and I'm about to end the call when an unfamiliar voice finally comes through.

"Miss Finnegan? I apologize for the broken connection. The location I'm calling from is most certainly at fault. This is Saint Tanner, on behalf of the military. Do you have a moment?"

My words get stuck in my throat, and my knees buckle so suddenly I have to sit down.

"Miss Finnegan?"

"Yes. Hello. How can I help you?"

I don't ask him how he has my number, or what he wants. If anything, this is probably something to do with my dead brother, since that's the only reason the military has ever contacted me in any way, shape, or form. But to reach out now, after all these years...

"I have the commander on a secure line. He wants to speak with you. May I transfer you over?"

My eyes round at the corners in shock.

"E-Excuse me?" I breathe out, my entire world spinning. I'm sent into a daze I'm failing to control.

"Commander Rowan King is on a secure line. May I—"

"No, I heard you. I'm just... Yes, I'll take the call."

This isn't happening. How the hell is this happening?

The line breaks for a split second before I hear it snap back in place on a different connection. My heart leaps to my throat, and my legs quiver. What do I say?

What the hell do I say to this man? He's a real person now, no longer just a ghost in my fantasies. And I have no idea how to deal with that fact.

"Hello, Dove," he says, his deep voice searing along my nerve endings, making me press my thighs together behind my desk. *Oh, God.*

I run a nervous hand through my hair, trying to find my words.

"H-Hello."

"I..." he starts, and I clutch the phone tighter. "I know it's been years..."

My body burns for him, even here, even now, even when it's only his voice.

Jesus, Dove. Pull yourself together.

"I'm sorry," he finally says. "I wish I could've been there for you after Cole's death."

An old ache settles inside my chest, and I struggle to come up with anything to say.

"Cole was my best friend," he adds. "And my best lieutenant. I should've been there for his family when he died. Please forgive me for not being able to."

"His journals never made it back home with his belongings," I breathe out, looking out into the distance as I relive the memory. "I wish I knew what he was feeling... thinking... before he..."

"I have them. Here, at my house."

"Oh." I ponder the reason for that, face flushing hotter. "Is that..." I gulp. "Is that why we're on this call?"

He grunts—there's a moment of hesitation there, as if he shouldn't really have called me at all.

"No."

I nod absently, gripping my necklace.

"You know why I called, Dove," he says, his voice deepening two more octaves.

I can't breathe.

"It wasn't enough. Touching you that day... You felt like the most amazing fucking drug. It was intoxicating. And then I never tasted you again. Ever. Do you have any idea what that did to me?"

"Rowan," I whisper, and the word rolls off my tongue like butter on warm toast, as if saying it is as normal as breathing. This is our second conversation in five years, and yet I feel completely comfortable calling him by his first name. "What are you saying...?"

He can't possibly remember me like that.

He exhales in my ear, a breathy, needy sound, and I nearly whimper in response.

"In my dreams, when I fuck you, you call out my name every night. Raw, and needy, and dripping with want. It's the sweetest fucking sound I've heard in my life. But I need to hear it for real, Dove. Because if I don't, my sanity is simply going to snap. And I don't know..." He groans. "I don't know how else to deal with it. Not anymore."

"You don't mean that." I shake my head as my brows knit together in shock.

"I *do* mean that. And I intend to show you, in explicit detail, how I really wanted to touch you that day but couldn't." He sighs. "I know a lot of time has passed. But to be completely honest, even if you don't feel the same way I do, that won't stop me from trying to make you mine."

Jesus Christ.

Gathering my thoughts, I pause, hearing only silence from the other side.

How can this happen? He's the Combatant Commander of the Army. He's fighting a war right now. And I'm just a girl from the suburbs who likes to imagine we're together from time to time.

What he's telling me is insane... and so is the fact that I'm considering it without really giving it much thought.

After all, even if this is about him quenching his thirst for one night... why shouldn't I explore it? Maybe it will show me he's not who I thought he'd be. And then I'd finally be freed from his spell. I could start seeing other men—normal men, like Jared, or the guy on the marketing team at Miss Pratt's law firm. Men I might have a shot at being in a relationship with, because they're just as regular as I am.

"I've had... dreams, too," I confess, keeping my voice low so nobody else hears me. "Dreams I couldn't talk to anyone about. I kept seeing you everywhere, feeling crazy for willingly refusing to leave the prison of the memory we both have. I still haven't moved on from it. And I don't understand..." I shake my head. "I don't understand why or how it happened. But I know there's no way I'm going to say no to seeing you again."

His breathing deepens, but it's still very much controlled. A stark contrast from mine that alternately keeps getting trapped in my lungs or coming out too fast.

"When can I see you, angel?" he asks.

Just then, Miss Pratt enters the room, and I have to pretend I'm not utterly turned on by the voice of the man on the other end of the line... and that my panties aren't drenched, and my face isn't flushing hot.

I hate this. I wish I had more time to speak with him, to hear that voice for as long as I can.

"Everything all right?" my boss asks absently. "Go home. I need you rested for court."

I only get to nod before she exits the room again, her lips thinning my way in a silent good bye.

"I'm... I'm sorry. That was my boss. I'm still at work," I tell Rowan. "I... could see you tonight. Right now, actually. Unless that's too short a notice. No, what am I saying? You're a really busy man. How about—"

"Right now? I was hoping you'd say that, so I wouldn't freak you out with my impatience."

I relax a little, leaning back in my chair. "Patience is not my strong suit either," I smile through the phone.

"Isn't it now?" He pauses, a hint of something dark hanging from his question. "I'm needed at the Aerospace Command Center tomorrow morning. Could I possibly get you to join me there?"

"Oh. Isn't that in another state? What was it..." I pause, trying to remember. "Minnesota?"

"Colorado," he gently corrects me. "We're flying there in an hour. And returning tomorrow morning. You don't have to worry about anything. All you have to do is come."

"So... an overnight stay."

"Correct."

"With... you."

"You and me. Alone, for the whole night... in Colorado. Yes." I can sense a smile when he speaks those words.

And then? What happens then?

I want to ask him, but I don't. It sounds like a total one-night stand, but fuck it. We're not part of the same world anyway. And I know I have to get this man out of my system before the longing starts to get the worst of me.

"Okay," I tell him. "Okay, I'd love to join you. Meet you at the airport, then?"

"Splendid. A car is already on the way to pick you up," he says, ignoring my question. "No need to go back home unless you want to. But I promise, you won't need anything you might be thinking to bring. Everything will be ready for you in Colorado."

"Why does this sound like you planned all of this before asking if I wanted to come?"

"Because I did. Because I've already decided that you're mine."

FOUR

The black SUV that picked me up stopped in the middle of a blocked and empty road. Graham—the driver—tells me Rowan's convoy would be here in a few minutes, so he can switch vehicles and we can go to the airport together.

I'm so nervous, I don't know what to do with myself. Graham eyes me in the rearview mirror every now and then. He's even asked me if I'm all right. I lied, of course, telling him I'm just tired from work. But exhaustion wouldn't really make someone shift in her seat every five seconds. Or rub my sweaty palms on my skirt more times than I can count. I would probably care more about what he thinks of my strange behavior if Rowan wasn't occupying every thought I have.

Just when I look out into the distance again, another black SUV approaches. I suck in a breath, pulse pounding loudly in my ears. I see even more cars behind the SUV that look exactly the same. Rowan could be sitting in any of them.

Fuck. I wonder if he's as nervous as I am, but it's hard to picture him losing control of his emotions. The man has gone to war. He has thousands of lives in the palms of his hands every day. His heart skipping a beat for a woman he wants to fuck tonight is most certainly not on his to-do list.

Most of the convoy passes us by, stopping a few feet ahead of us. But a new space between the cars has just been created. Knowing exactly what to do, Graham gets the SUV started again and makes a short U-turn to fit in the gap that's been left.

Then, for a few moments, time freezes in place.

The wind lashes against the blades of tall, uncut grass along the side of the road, bending them back and forth. But other than that simple, rhythmic motion, no one dares move a muscle.

The silence is deafening, and even I have stopped shifting in my seat. It's like a predator has just spotted me, and I'll have the best chances for survival if I just stay still.

The sound of a door opening gets my attention, but it's just Graham stepping out of the car and heading toward the last SUV in the convoy. He doesn't get in, but rather waits there, looking straight ahead like he's supposed to stay away from something. Like he's supposed to now stay away from *me*.

I'm all alone in here, and I know what's coming.

In the next few seconds, Rowan will be sitting next to me, and I'm supposed to pretend it's just another car ride like any other.

But it's not, though, is it? Because Rowan will see

me. After all these years, he'll see me. And I'll see him. And he will touch me. And I will burn, because what other way could my body react to his touch, if not by reducing itself to ashes because of how much he consumes me?

I turn my eyes to the left, where I can concentrate on the waving grass.

The silhouette of a man approaches the car I'm in. I'd been so lost in thought that I hadn't even seen him when he was farther away.

I hear the door when it opens. All I see is his torso, and the strong arm that presses down against the seat next to me.

The leather sighs softly under his weight.

The space yields to his presence with a quiet grace.

And then—

"Hello, angel," he says in a voice so low and endearing that my whole body turns to face him despite my nerves. As if it now decided I'm no longer its master, but Rowan is instead.

"Rowan..."

His eyes meet mine, and I forget everything else around me.

Last time I saw him, he had just turned 27. I looked him up on the Internet a couple of weeks after we met. The five years that passed since then have only made him look more sleek... like fine steel.

Now, at 32, his presence oozes with masculine power and authority. His shoulders are wider, muscles even more defined, and his eyes... fuck, those eyes could silence me with just one quick glance if they wanted to.

"You look beautiful," he says, drawing a real smile out of me.

I don't even think about the nine hours of work I put in today. Or about the fact that I had almost zero time to retouch my makeup or even change my clothes.

From the way he looks at me, I know he's not lying. If he thinks I'm beautiful right now, then that's what I am. I am whatever he wants me to be.

"I'm really, really nervous," I blurt out.

He smiles, and it reminds me of the way he did it that day, when he first saw me.

"And I'm really fucking desperate for you. Come here, angel."

He cups my face with his callused hands and brings me in, pressing his mouth to mine. His lips are soft, and the kiss is gentle in the beginning. He smells so masculine—of leather, pine, and that muted undertone of a scent I never managed to figure out.

He groans, and I swallow down the sound before his tongue darts out, pushing against the seam of my mouth. I open up for him, a whimper traveling from my throat to his, as I dip my head backward to let him devour me. He tastes like fresh morning dew on mint leaves in the valley. I lean into his mouth, chasing more of it. Chasing all of it.

Instinctively, I place my hands on his forearms, feeling his muscles clench behind his uniform jacket. But it's not enough. I want to touch every part of him. So I place my fingers on his chest instead. He seems to want the exact same thing, and lowers his hands to my thighs as goose bumps start to pebble every inch square of my skin.

He wants me. He wants me just as much as I want him, if not more.

I smile against his lips, and he pauses, huffing out deep breaths as he stares me down with his brows slightly furrowed.

"You taste better than I could've ever imagined. What should we do with you, hmm?"

"Rowan... I'm so... please, you have to..."

I don't even know what I'm asking him. I just want him to take me. Right here, surrounded by all these other men who are waiting for us in their designated cars.

I don't care about anyone or anything else right now.

"Be a good girl and take these off for me," he says, his fingers dipping under my skirt, tugging at the edges of my panties until they slide down to the middle of my thighs. I hoist myself up, leaning into him so he can take them off completely.

"Lie back. Let me see you."

Heart fluttering and nerves swarming low in my belly, I do as he says, propping my back against the door and shyly spreading my legs. He drags a hand down his face, and I wait for his next command.

"No. Open for me, angel. Wider."

I exhale a shaky breath, parting my legs a bit more. I know it's probably not enough, but the way he rakes his eyes over me—with so much hunger—makes me feel overanalyzed. Exposed.

His hands suddenly hook around my ankles and,

with one swift movement, he lifts up my legs, balancing them on his shoulders. I gasp, holding onto the seat in front of me for stability.

"What a pretty little cunt," he says, pulling my skirt up to rest on my stomach and revealing me entirely to him. "Exquisite."

I squirm and wiggle my hips against the seat, my pussy throbbing at the praise caressing it.

"Did I tell you to move?"

"N-No."

"Stay still, angel. I want to kiss you some more."

"Y-Yes. Please, Rowan..."

Nerves pounding inside my skin, I close my eyes, impatient to feel the touch of his lips on mine.

I can feel the weight of his body pressing down into the seat as he leans forward. I can feel his rough hands trailing up my thighs. But what I don't expect to feel is his warm breath tickling my most sensitive spot.

My eyes snap open in shock.

"Y-You said you were going to kiss me."

His lips make contact with my pussy. I shudder, feeling the dark smile on his face stretching them out.

"I am."

His tongue darts out, warm and velvety, pushing against my entrance. I've never had anyone go down on me before. I've never had anyone do *any* of this stuff to me before. It's dirty and intrusive, and it feels a million times better than anything else I've done by myself in my room.

I moan, dipping my head backward as my face scrunches under the intense sensation of being fucked with his tongue. But as soon as I feel his fingers nearing my other hole, my eyes snap open in shock once again.

"Not there," I plead, shame causing red patches all over my cheeks. "I've never..."

"Yes, there. Relax for me. I've got you."

He doesn't wait for me to say anything else before he dives back in and swirls his perfect tongue against my throbbing clit. My legs start shaking of their own accord, and when he pushes the tip of his finger inside my ass, I crumble completely. I have no choice but to come on his tongue right there.

My entire body is spasming, almost making me fall off the back seat completely. But Rowan pins me down with his free arm, and I let the waves of my release wash over me one by one. I call out his name, grinding against his mouth as I squeeze every last drop of pleasure from this moment.

"So fucking sweet..." He trails off, placing kisses up along my bare legs. "I wish we could keep going. There are so many things I want to do to you. But we've got to get on that plane. And then... when we're alone again, later tonight—"

"I know. That was... amazing," I breathe out, still trying to regain my composure. "But before we leave, I'd really like to pay back the favor..."

He cuts me a stern look that has me pulling myself up to a sitting position.

"You think that was for you?"

"Well, you... you made me..."

"That was all for *my* pleasure, angel. I don't need you to do anything for me."

I'm not sure what that means—it can't possibly have been for his own pleasure. He made *me* come. Surely he must want to have his own release. Back when we were in college, Sterling always used to say that if a guy goes down on you, you reciprocate. Always.

"I want this over your pretty legs until we arrive at the airport," Rowan says, sliding his uniform jacket off his shoulders, and laying it across my skirt and thighs. "Is that understood?"

"Oh, God, is the skirt too short? I'm sorry if I dressed inappropriately for this. I didn't know—"

Says the girl who just showed him her pussy, I think to myself.

"The skirt is perfect. We're just not done here, you and I."

Before I get to ask what he means, he adds, "I'm calling Graham back in. Behave," he smirks. Why would he assume I won't be nice around Graham?

But I fix up my hair, and he licks the rest of my release off his lips, groaning as his senses register the taste once more. The action is so dirty and erotic that it makes my thighs press together.

Graham gets back in the driver's seat, and he looks more focused than ever. It's as if Rowan's presence here is now turning up the pressure tenfold for him. I'm just glad he doesn't look like he knows what happened in this car before he came back in.

The convoy gets going again, car by car, until we're moving in a single line toward the airport. And as Graham talks with the other drivers in his earpiece, Rowan sprawls his arm across my thighs, under the jacket he placed above them, and dips his middle finger inside my pussy.

I gasp, breath shivering from the pleasure building up almost immediately inside my walls. I turn my head toward him and see him raise his eyebrows in warning.

Behave, he told me. And now I suddenly understand why.

My pussy clenches around his finger and I get the urge to grind myself on it. He sees it, and lowers his head in my direction, whispering, "I licked this pussy. It's mine now. And I'm going to keep my finger in there for as long as I want. So be quiet, stay still, and enjoy the ride. Yes?"

"Rowan..." I whimper, pleading with him with my eyes not to torture me like this.

His finger remains unmoving, trapped inside my pussy like he has no intention of ever releasing me. Like that's where it belongs. My muscles continue to clench around it, and I know by looking into his eyes that this is going to be the most torturous half an hour of my life.

FIVE

The clink of a glass touching wood wakes me up. I'm in the hotel suite Rowan booked for us in Colorado Springs, where he instructed me to eat, sleep, and wait for him in our bed while he met with the Deputy Director of Operations at the command center. I barely had it in me to eat anything at all from all the nerves, but he said something about there being consequences. And because we didn't have much time to talk about it in detail, I figured I'd be better off doing what he asked.

Besides... I think... I think I like doing what he says. Listening to his commands. Pleasing him to draw praise and affection from him. It's like a game where all I have to do is be a good girl for him, and he'll give me anything I want. Easy enough.

The room is lit, and I see Rowan place a glass of something that looks expensive down on the nightstand.

My heart starts pounding harder in my chest, but I

don't get up. I let him come to me instead, simply because I think if I tried, I wouldn't be able to walk toward him. My legs wouldn't work at this moment.

I fist my hands in the covers as I feel his eyes assessing me again. It's not any less intimidating than earlier in the car or on the private plane. Except here... it really is just the two of us. No one waiting for us, or demanding any more of his time.

"You ate," he confirms, dropping his military jacket to the floor and rolling up the sleeves of the shirt beneath it. "You slept. And you waited for me in our bed, just like I asked."

"Yes," I gasp.

"Good. I want you to keep doing that. Listen to my commands. Do you think you can?"

I nod, my pussy throbbing with need and begging to be touched.

Like a panther moving through tall grass, Rowan stalks closer to me, until he's hovering right above me. He found me—the predator found me, and now there's no escaping his deadly fangs. He looks like he's about to devour me. And I make no effort to deny him the prey he hunted down.

His eyes roam over my body, darkening with the claws of the demons residing inside... as if they're now crawling out of him, licking their lips in anticipation to take a bite.

"You shouldn't have agreed to come here," he says absently, trailing his knuckles up my bare legs.

"I wanted to."

"You should ask me to take you back." His fingers

touch the crease between my thigh and my pussy, pushing a trembling exhale out of my lungs.

"You don't scare me," I lie, letting out a nervous, hushed laugh.

I might only know Rowan from the news articles I read about him, but he was Cole's best friend. And he comforted me that day when he gave me the news of his death. He's not going to hurt me. He's not—

"Pity." He presses the tips of his fingers into my warm pussy, through the thin layer of my panties. I showered and changed into new ones when I got to the hotel suite and saw they were laid out on the bed for me. I moan softly, then quickly close my mouth shut. "Though I promise you'll scream when I start taking what's mine. Because you *are* mine now, aren't you, angel?"

"F-For tonight," I whisper, feeling my pussy drench my panties in the exact spot he's touching me.

He peels his gaze off my body to meet my eyes with another one of those stern looks that has me trapping the air in my lungs "We're going to have to fix that."

"What?"

"Your self-doubt."

I close my eyes, my body arching for him, needing him like I need my next breath of air.

"It wasn't hard to hear it in your voice when you told me you'd come. You think I called you in for a quick fuck?" he drawls, sliding two fingers inside me through my panties, denying me the feel of his skin rubbing against my walls. With his other hand, he squeezes my cheeks together, pursing my lips and making me open my eyes again. "No, no, no, angel," he smiles.

His fingers scissor inside me, pushing deeper, and deeper, until the panties get so wet I can practically feel the pads of his fingers and the creases of his knuckles sliding in and out. I part my thighs for him while he makes sure there's no way I can escape his questioning eyes.

My face flushes hotter at the gesture. It's too intimate—way too intimate for two strangers who got together for just one night. But he doesn't seem to care about any of that.

"This skin. This *scent*," he groans. "I've gone years trying to remember every single detail of how fucking good you felt in my arms. My hunger runs deeper than whatever you are willing to offer me tonight. I'll have you now. And I'll have you tomorrow. And I won't be able to let go after that, even if I tried."

Hand still in my pussy, Rowan's nostrils flare as he stares me down—raw and vulnerable, and fully at his mercy. My whole body trembles when he slides his fingers out of me, leaving me empty and wanton. I want to beg him not to stop, but I'm scared... ashamed of what he might think of me if I do.

"Besides..." He hooks his fingers behind the edges of my panties, slowly pulling them down to my knees. "I bet this gorgeous pink pussy would enjoy being worshipped more than once. Am I wrong?"

"Please." The word comes out against my will, as molten need burns through me and through the sheets under my body. I've never realized just how much of me Rowan claimed that day when he held me. Right now, it very much feels like he claimed it all.

"Pick a safe word first, angel. I need to be careful with you."

Christ.

"A safe word," I nod, biting my lower lip, "Is... is the word 'pink' good enough?"

I blush, knowing that the word came from what he said earlier—about my pink pussy wanting to be worshipped.

A moan echoing from his chest tells me the chosen word will do as his attention returns to my pussy. "Say it anytime you want, and everything stops. No matter what we're doing. Do you understand?"

I nod, though I don't really understand. I'll never want him to stop.

"What a good girl. So sweet and eager to please me. But I do think something's missing. Do you know what it is?"

I shake my head against the pillow.

"Take off my belt."

"M-Me?" I whimper. I don't think I feel confident enough to do that.

His hand comes to the top of my head, caressing my hair in gentle strokes.

"Take off my belt, angel. Don't make me ask again."

I gulp, getting up higher against the headboard as I pull the leather strap through his belt loops with trembling hands.

"Around your pretty neck now."

I hesitate initially, but I'm not about to call out my

safe word just yet. Not until I get a real taste of him—until I know what he's really made of.

"Just like that. Here, let me help you," he says, the warmth of his hands against my sensitive skin as he works the strap through the buckle, fastening it as tight as it can go around my neck. It's already hard to breathe, but the forceful sensation is doing something to me... it's making my body come alive for him.

"Rowan..." I utter, my eyes open wide from struggling to breathe as he smiles down on me.

"Tell me your safe word, and I'll remove it right now."

It's not easy, but after calming myself down, I manage to take back control of my lungs, even under the pressure of the belt. So I just shake my head, feeling my pussy drip with arousal across my thighs.

"No? Then let's get you out of bed. On your knees."

Like a genie newly released from a bottle, I obey my new master, draping my legs over the edge of the bed and lowering myself to the floor until my knees feel the hardness of the boards.

Rowan takes the leftover belt hanging around my neck, pulling it up like a leash, until it tightens just a bit more on my flesh. My pussy pulses at the action, and I try to hide my blush by lowering my gaze.

"I'm going to go into the kitchen. And you're going to crawl, following me around, until I get you some sweet relief for your aching little cunt. Is that understood?"

"Y-Yes. Yes, sir," I mutter. I don't know how I addressed him like that, but I don't dare call out his name again. I expected a lot of the man who has haunted my dreams for so long, but this? I never expected him to be so intense. So... in control, and sure of himself.

He starts walking, tugging on the leash just enough to get my knees moving. I get down on my hands, lifting my gaze to see the backs of his suited thighs walking in front of me. I'm so wet, I can feel the normal air temperature caressing my pussy through the drenched panties as if it's ten degrees cooler than it actually is. It's a small relief, but I need so much more than air caressing me against my throbbing clit.

Reaching the open-space kitchen feels like an eternity and a half. But when we do, Rowan opens the door to the freezer, pulling out a small tray of ice. He flips it up, making the cubes fall flat onto his opened palm before he closes the door and turns to face me.

"Open," he commands, pointing an ice cube at my mouth.

I stick my tongue out, but he doesn't immediately place it there. Instead, he just looks at me for a few moments with that same hunger flashing in his eyes.

"So fucking pretty. I could watch you like this forever."

I smile at the praise, my tongue still out as saliva builds up in my mouth. I want to close it, but I don't think I'm allowed yet.

"Now," he says, placing the first ice cube in my mouth. It's cold and wet, and I can already feel it melting, droplets of water sliding down along the sides of my tongue.

He lets go of the leash he improvised, and brings his index finger under my chin, lifting it up.

"Hold this in your mouth while you crawl to the couch. You'll have to be fast. Because if it melts before I get to push it inside your pussy, you'll give me no choice but to spank that beautiful ass. Do you understand?"

"Yesh," I say, the word slipping out awkwardly past my opened lips.

"Good girl," he smiles, then lets go of my chin.

I close my mouth, rushing to the couch that's only a few feet away from us. He wants to... spank me? God. What is this man made of? And how is he making my pussy pulse with just his words and nothing else?

I get up on the couch, sitting on my heels and pushing the ice cube back out on my tongue. The more it stays inside my mouth, the faster it will melt. I'm not even sure how much of it is left at this point.

Rowan, on the other hand, seems to be taking his sweet time as he collects a few more ice cubes before finally making his way toward me. Taking a seat next to me, he taps his lap and says, "Come here. Give me your pussy."

Fuck. I whimper in anticipation and shame as I go to sit on his lap, the position so intimate it makes my cheeks flush. I've never held him before. Never felt the wall of muscle beneath his shirt other than that one minute five years ago. I want to lean into it, I want my hands to roam all over his body, but it doesn't seem like I get a say in it just yet. Plus, the ice cube is fucking melting.

I lie back on the couch, positioned with my hips in his lap. His hand tugs at the white, lacy undergarments he bought me and rips them open to expose my swollen pussy.

"There. Now open your mouth and give me back the ice."

There's not much left of it at this point. But I sprawl out my tongue and he takes it, the warmth of his fingers clashing with the coldness of my lips.

Without any warning, he places the ice in the middle of my clit, pushing it with his finger as I arch my back and gasp out a moan.

"Quiet," he commands, letting the ice slide down, then pushing it inside my pussy. "I'm not anywhere close to being done, and you're distracting me with your pretty moans."

What is he doing to me? What is this man doing to me—ahh.

I melt down into the couch, biting my lip to stop from crying out.

My pussy swallows up the cube, and I can feel it melt down inside the warmth of my walls. It slides against them, making me move my hips up and down.

Another cube makes it inside me, Rowan's finger smearing me with both my wetness and the melted water. They slide in easily, cooling me down, but making practically no difference in how utterly aroused I am.

"Please, please, just..." I plead, but the rest of the sentence trails off. Why isn't he fucking me already? Why is he torturing me like this?

"You want more, angel?"

"Yes, yes, I—"

"You haven't earned it yet, I'm afraid. You'll take what I'm giving you for now."

I close my eyes and he pushes past the folds of my dripping pussy, entering me as far as his fingers can go, until they touch whatever ice is left in my channel. As soon as I feel him inside, I moan so loudly I have to bite my lip to quiet down.

My eyes crack open when he pinches my nipple between his fingers. I arch and I wiggle and I whimper-moan, his sleek fingers sliding in and out of me with ease.

"That's it. That's my good girl," he whispers, his other hand moving from my breasts to my neck, pulling on the belt and taking away my air. "Don't come yet, angel. Hold on for little bit longer," he says, his fingers stuck inside me as I struggle to breathe through an incoming orgasm.

The pain around my neck isn't helping—it's turning up the pleasure tenfold—and I'm this close to coming all over his hand and lap. "Breathe for me. Hold it," he says, finally releasing the belt.

"Jesus..." I moan, taking huge breaths of air as my pussy clenches around him, begging me to come. "I can't. I can't—"

"Rowan," he says, sliding another finger down into my ass. "That's the only name you'll scream when I fuck you."

My orgasm explodes like a tsunami, sending shockwaves all throughout my flushed body. At the same time, Rowan's hand thrusts faster, both in my pussy and in my ass, making me lose complete control of myself. I come all over his thigh, clenching down on his fingers, a trickle of sweat beading my forehead from the intensity of it.

"So fucking perfect. So beautiful," he praises as I twitch under his hands.

"Rowan..." I mewl.

"You did so well, angel."

"I'm sorry. I couldn't wait."

But he isn't angry. Or disappointed. Or disinterested in the slightest. Instead, he smiles and starts working on my overstimulated clit with his thumb again. "We have all night to work on that."

"I don't think... I don't think I can do that again."

"Oh, but you will. You'll come over my tongue and hands for as long as it takes to quench my thirst for tonight. And then tomorrow, we'll go again. And again. And again. Until you're a pleading mess covered in cum and drool, and begging for my cock."

After showering together and making me come more times than I can count, my back is pressed against Rowan's chest as he cradles me in bed. I'm numb—my pussy is numb, my nipples are overstimulated, and my ass feels like he's already fucked it with everything he's got. I wince at knowing he hasn't even truly started.

The sheets no longer smell just like me, from when I waited for him earlier—they smell like us. And I can't help but let a sheepish smile spread on my face at the fact.

He's real. This is real.

And so is the erection caging my ass from behind.

Rowan caresses my hair, breathing me in as he groans into my pebbled skin.

"I can't believe you're finally mine. It's been so lonely, Dove. So fucking hard thinking of you but knowing I couldn't have you."

"I know," I murmur. "I thought about you for so long, Rowan..."

"So when did you stop?"

"What?"

"You said it in past tense. So when did you stop thinking about me?"

Oh. I pause, gathering my thoughts, while he hugs me tighter into his naked chest.

"I thought... I thought it was insane. Thinking about you like that. You were a fantasy I'd made up in my mind. I had to let you go, Rowan, I didn't think you'd—"

"I'm glad I wasn't too late, angel. That's all I care about."

"I don't think I ever really gave you up. You were always there, in the back of my mind. All you had to do was show up..." I smile.

He presses a kiss to my head, and my legs go weak.

But when silence drifts in between us, my thoughts torment me instead. What happens now? Will he just call me in to fuck me whenever he feels like it, while I go about my life? Will he want to see me again after tonight?

Doubt creeps in and my body goes taut in his arms.

"I, um... I have to go," I say. "Early in the morning."

"No, you don't."

"Yes," I press on. "It's about my job. I have to be at court on Monday, and there are still things I need to prepare tomorrow…"

"Cancel it," he says, very matter-of-fact.

I turn around, facing the sleepy, sexy-as-fuck face of the most important man in the country right now.

"I can't," I laugh, my confidence slowly returning. "Miss Pratt would kill me. And then you wouldn't be able to do what you just did to me tonight."

He scoffs, smiling with closed eyes. "You underestimate me, angel. Being bat-shit crazy was a prerequisite for earning the highest rank in the military."

"Sure it was," I laugh.

"Who's the judge taking your case on Monday?"

"It's Miss *Pratt's* case—and I can't tell you that. You just told me you're bat-shit crazy. What are you going to do? Kill the woman?"

Another smile, and a kiss that lands on my nose this time.

"Answer me."

"Judge Lydia Davis."

"Okay," he turns over to the nightstand to get his phone, the sheets rustling with him.

"What are you doing…?" I ask, a concerned scowl on my face. "Rowan!"

"Quiet, angel. I'm working."

I watch in shock and awe as Rowan dials a number on his phone, pinching his eyebrows together as he squeezes his eyes shut to readjust to the light.

"Yes, hello. This is Commander Rowan King. I'm sorry to disturb you at this hour—"

"Rowan," I whisper-shout, but he brings his finger to his mouth, tapping his lips while giving me a stern look.

"There's a case on Monday under Judge Davis— Lydia Davis. Yes, I need it postponed. To..." He looks at me. "Friday?"

I give him a blank stare. I can't believe him right now!

"No, that wouldn't work actually," he resumes. "Can you— Yeah? Perfect. Thank you. Have a good night."

"Rowan!" I get up to a seated position, anger and shame and, I guess, a fuzzy feeling coursing through me all at once. "You can't just do that. That's abuse of power!"

"No point in having power if you can't abuse it from time to time." He puts his phone back on the nightstand. "You're sleeping with me tonight. And tomorrow. And the night after that. Period."

"Rowan..."

"What's the matter, angel?"

My phone dings on the other nightstand, and I lean over to swipe it open while Rowan grabs my naked ass from behind. I bite my lip in response, but I'm glad he can't see it right now. I'm mad at him. And I need him to understand.

"It's Miss Pratt. She just said..." I shake my head. "Our case has gotten postponed to next Tuesday."

"Perfect. I love it when things move fast in this

country," he smirks.

"Rowan! You can't just do that. People were planning for this trial. It's not right..."

"A billionaire and a rival corporation? *Please*," he scoffs. "They have enough money already. They can wait until next Tuesday while I fuck my girl at least a couple more times."

"And then what?" I scowl. "I go back and you call me in whenever you feel like it again?"

Not the time, or the place.

Fuck, Dove, you're fucking this up.

Stupid, stupid, stupid.

But Rowan's face doesn't falter. Nor does it tense up. Which is why I don't expect it at all when he turns over to face me, grabbing my neck and squeezing tight enough for all the air to come out.

"I told you we were going to fix it, but I didn't think we'd have to start in the middle of the night. Your self-doubt is going to have to go, Dove. Because my good little angel is perfect, and I will not allow her to degrade herself like that. Nod if you understand."

I nod. I fucking nod, butterflies coming to life in my belly and in my pussy.

"Good. Now." He squeezes harder, and I reach down to touch my already pulsing clit. "Nuh-uh-uh. Take your hand out of your cunt. You're not touching it again until I say so. And right now, you're going to sleep like the good girl I know you are. And in the morning, if I'm feeling generous, I might play with your ass a little bit until I let you come. Do. You. Understand?"

I nod hard and fast. His hand is still wrapped around my neck, my lungs about to explode from the lack of oxygen. He smirks, releasing me, and I take in huge heaps of air like I've never breathed before in my life.

He presses me to his chest once more, his head resting on top of mine.

"Sleep well, angel," he says, while I blink hard and fast through whatever the hell just happened.

It's at this moment that I realize... Rowan King is not my hero, as younger me would've thought.

He's my monster. And now I serve under his command.

SIX

When I wake up, I spread my fingers across Rowan's side of the bed—a cold, empty mess of sheets. And I can't help but wonder if all of last night has been nothing but a dream, just like the many others I've had of him.

But I scan my eyes around the room, and I know it wasn't. His scent still lingers all over me—of leather and pine—and I bask in it like a cat kneading in soft cushions.

Last night was... intense. He had me wrapped around his finger with his low voice and his demeaning orders that made me want to beg for more of him. And that tongue. *God*, that tongue...

My pussy jolts awake at the memory, and I bite my lip, wondering why he isn't here to make good on the promise he mentioned before we fell asleep. I drape my legs over the mattress and pick up Rowan's immaculate shirt from yesterday that I find tossed across one of the armchairs. I walk out into the hallway while buttoning it all the way down.

The hotel suite has quite a bunch of rooms, and I have no idea where to even look for him. But it doesn't take long before butterflies come to life in my stomach at the sound of his voice coming from one of them. I can't help my smile from spreading across on my face.

He's here. And he's mine. And—

"Kill them all," he says, dragging a silent gasp out of me.

I press myself to the wall next to what seems to be his temporary office, shock spreading through my body. I don't dare move a muscle or make a noise. Because I know, even if we've just reconnected, that what I've just heard isn't the voice of *my* Rowan. It's the voice of the Commander himself.

"With all due respect, Commander, this would cause massive backlash if it somehow got out," another voice answers. A voice that's not too soft, but not too tense either—as if the man wants to take control of the situation, but Rowan's mind keeps pushing against his own, never giving him the opportunity to do so.

"Backlash is the least of my concerns, Sergeant. We want to win this war, not bat our eyelashes to the public for sympathy."

"But if it gets out..."

"Then make sure it *doesn't*. Excuse me one moment— Angel, stop hiding like a little mouse and come sit with me," he hollers, and my heart leaps to my throat.

Fuck.

"I...um... I'm not decent right now."

"Even better." I can practically see the dark smile etching across his face.

"I'm sorry," I'm quick to say, "I didn't mean to interrupt. I'll make myself scarce until you—"

"Dove," he growls, and goose bumps pebble my skin as my body registers the low vibrations of his voice. "If I wanted you to leave, I'd have said so. Come here. I won't ask again."

With shallow breaths I walk through the doorframe, my cheeks burning with shame as I come face-to-face with Rowan. He's sitting at a huge mahogany desk, all dressed up, talking to another man whose uniform doesn't show a single crease.

"Don't be shy, angel. Sergeant Rhames won't bite."

But I *am* shy. I am so fucking shy, and the thought of another man seeing me walk in wearing nothing but Rowan's shirt makes me want to disappear into thin air. It also makes me horny as fuck.

As quietly and quickly as possible, I tiptoe to Rowan's side of the desk until I finally see the face of this other man. He's tall and muscular, his skin a russet, reddish-brown color. And he doesn't look uncomfortable at all to see me—as if he's used to Rowan's ways and insanity.

Or as if... Rowan's done this before. With other women. The thought sends daggers through my heart but I try to remain unfazed as Rowan extends his hand toward me and pulls me in.

"Perfect," he says, offering up praises while looking me up and down with a smile. "Be a good girl and sit quietly while I finish this conversation."

I look around, but there's no other chair. Where does he want me to sit?

"On your knees, angel."

Oh, fuck.

My cheeks flush and my pussy clenches, eager to please him in whichever way he wants. Sergeant Rhames doesn't react, though I try my hardest to avoid his stare.

I could call in my safe word. *Pink*—I could say it right now if I wanted to. But I don't. Whatever Rowan has got planned for me today, I want all of it. I want to lick my plate clean.

"Okay," I whisper, lowering myself to my knees at his feet, the desk hiding my face away. The only view I get is that of the wood and the polished floor under my ass.

Rowan's hand comes down and rests on the top of my head, his fingers gently digging into my hair, caressing it—caressing *me*. The action is soft and endearing and unlike anything else I've experienced as a grown adult. There's something deeply erotic about being touched like this, every movement of his fingers charged with dark, delicious promise.

"Beautiful, isn't she?" he asks, and Sergeant Rhames lets out a short chuckle.

"Very," he agrees, a hint of something odd in his tone as he continues, "I would call you a lucky bastard if you weren't my boss."

I hold my breath at the sound of that, expecting Rowan to strangle this man for the way he just spoke to him. And I'm not the only one doing that—for a few moments, it feels as if the entire room has become sentient and stopped breathing.

But Rowan doesn't react like that. Instead, I feel his body shake with a low laugh as he continues to caress my hair under the table.

"That I am, Sergeant. Now... please go and execute my orders, and watch over this operation yourself. Don't answer any questions on my behalf. If anyone wants to challenge this decision, they know how to reach me. Is that understood?"

More silence, save for the weight of Sergeant Rhames moving from one leg to the other.

Rowan's hand stops in my hair, and for some reason *I* am the one feeling nervous over this whole thing. I can practically feel the tension wafting over in the air like a winter blanket of snow.

"Is. That. Understood?"

"Yes, sir," he finally says, and I can see Rowan tilting his head, observing him with a subtle smile lifting in the corner of his mouth. The kind you definitely don't want to be around.

Then Sergeant Rhames's feet start moving away from the desk, and I breathe out my nerves when I realize he's gone, my body going loose under Rowan's touch.

"Good morning, angel. Sleep well?"

I look up at him with big, concerned eyes, nodding softly as I meet his stare.

"I was kind of hoping you'd walk in here naked, the way I left you in our bed. But since you chose to wear my shirt instead of yours, I can't be too mad about it."

Our bed.

"But then Sergeant Rhames..." I mumble. "He would've seen me. All of me."

"Yes," he smiles. "And he would've hated me even more than he does. Because he can't have you, angel. No one else can."

My nipples harden at the dominance in his voice, and a whimper drags out of my throat. If he wants to share me, he will. If he wants to keep me away from everyone else, he will. Whatever he wants to do, he will do it. All the while my heart and my body keep on telling him *yes*.

"I quite like the sight of you on your knees," he grunts, his hand wrapping around the back of my neck. "Are you comfortable?"

"Yes," I say in a hushed tone. "I like it too. I like following your orders."

His eyes soften for just a moment before he drags his free hand over his face.

"Where have you been all my life, angel? You're everything I've ever wanted. You know that?"

I smile, his hand tightening on my neck possessively. Until I remember—

"Rowan?"

"Hmm?"

"What was all that about? Is the war starting again?"

"The war never truly ended, angel."

"But the press... they're saying..."

"The press is lying. There was a short time frame where it looked like we'd won. But unfortunately, things are rarely that straightforward."

"Oh."

"You don't need to worry. I've got you. You're mine now, Dove. And as long as I breathe, nothing's going to happen to you. Do you believe that?"

I nod, though it's hard not to worry. It's been a hard few years for everyone when the war was at its height. I've had my suspicions about the press lying to us, since we've been told over and over on TV that the small attacks still taking place in the Ridge were nothing to worry about.

"Not very convincing. Come here," he says, patting his leg as if he's calling a pet onto his lap.

I rotate my body to face him, the warmth of his hand sliding off the back of my neck as he follows my movements with his eyes. I get up on wobbly feet and carefully lower myself on his thigh, his hand sliding up to my naked pussy, fingers just barely dipping into my folds.

"Oh," I echo, as I watch his hand tease me.

A dark smile. "*Oh* is right," he says. "What's your safe word?"

"P-Pink."

"Good. I want to start training you today, angel."

Train me? Train me for what?

He senses my confusion and he adds, "I want your pussy wet for me when you hear my footsteps come home or when you smell my cologne in an empty room of this house. I want you wet and needy even when you're sleeping, so I can use your holes at any time I want. I want your body and mind to understand that I own you now. I mean that literally—in the real sense of the word. Unless, Dove, you want to break this off because it's too much. I don't want that, but I would *completely* understand—"

"No." I shake my head, my breathing shallow and my pussy throbbing with need. "It's not too much. I want this—I want *you*. I'll do whatever you want. Please, Rowan."

"Angel," he coos, caressing my pussy. "You have no idea what you're agreeing to. But when you start realizing it, please just know that your safe word is always here to protect you. Do you understand?"

"I won't need it," I shoot back, spreading my legs ever so slightly.

"You will. Say it. Tell me you understand."

"Yes," I whimper when his hand stops moving, getting my attention back on his words. "Yes, I understand."

"Good girl." He groans, lifting himself up while he pushes my torso onto his desk, my bare ass now facing him. "I want you to climb up on this desk and spread your knees apart. Show me everything, angel. Show me everything that's mine, so I can start taking it."

SEVEN

I pull my torso higher onto the cold desk, spreading my knees and opening up my pussy the way he wants me. A low hum of approval rumbles from his chest. My face is pressed against the sturdy wood as I try to anticipate where he'll claim me first. The sound of a zipper coming undone makes me swallow down my nerves. I wish I could see him—naked, raw, and throbbing just like I am.

But where I'm exposing every hole and every imperfection of my body to him, he's still dressed and controlling me like a puppet master. And I know that even if he hasn't said it, this is just another way to exert his dominance. That I'm the one who's been debauched, and he's the man who owns me.

He pushes a finger inside me, probing me, but it slides in easily. It seems to make him satisfied. The warmth of his cock then cages my pussy from behind, making me shudder when our bodies make contact.

This is the first time I've had sex since that stupid

one-night stand with Jared to help me get over the idea of ever being with Rowan. It didn't work, *obviously*, and now I regret not having waited for him. But at the very least, I understand what's expected of me with sex.

Jared made sure to tell me that I shouldn't just lie there like a log because it's boring and men don't like it. Remembering that, I arch myself backward, pressing my pussy to Rowan's erection and wiggling my ass at him. I let out a soft moan as well, wanting to make sure he's enjoying this too, not just me.

But before I get to do that again—

Smack.

Sharp pain spreads across my ass cheeks as tears quickly form at the backs of my eyes.

Did he...? He spanked me. He fucking *spanked* me.

"Stay still and take it the way I give it to you," he growls, wrapping one arm around the back of my neck. "You're not the one in control here, angel."

"Y-Yes. Yes, sir."

My pussy clenches around the crown of his cock, leaking out with arousal from the pain that still courses through my nerve endings. Fresh tears coat my eyelashes, binding them together. I want to wipe them away, but my hands are stuck at my sides, holding my pussy up in offering.

"Do not make me turn this ass red. I'd rather you cry from my cock gagging that pretty throat."

I think I nod in response, but I'm so lost in his words and in that voice that I don't even know what I'm doing anymore. Inch by inch, as if wanting to make sure I remember my safe word, he spears my pussy with his erection, pushing past my folds and sliding in between my walls until I feel the opened zipper making contact with my ass.

I close my eyes, focusing on the way my pussy stretches itself to the max, trying to adjust to the size of him. It hurts, but the pleasure is quick to replace the pain. I melt down into the desk, feeling every bulging vein and the soft skin on his hard cock.

"Now tell me, angel, has this pussy ever been fucked?" he asks as he caresses my ass.

"No," I gasp, immediately understanding what he means. I've had sex before—but I've never been fucked. Not the way he's about to do it. "No, sir."

He's inside me. And I can't stop clamping down on him.

I want him to start moving. I want him to take me. I want—

Smack.

My skin burns again, but this time, I'm chasing the pain like a junkie.

"Mmm, but that's not good, you see. Because I'm about to fuck this sweet cunt like it's my last time."

I don't even get to tell him to do it. As soon as the sentence is over, Rowan pulls himself out of me, and the next thrust is so brutal and fast it sends me a few inches higher on his desk. I cry out, his fingers digging into my neck, bruising me, claiming me. My eyes roll to the back of my head, then turn to him, his gaze meeting mine. He's hungry. They tell me that much.

I try my best to relax, to stay still, and let him use me the way he needs. But every thrust brings tendrils of pleasure that make my legs twitch and my pussy tighten.

I feel so alive. He takes my breath away.

"You," he breathes out, grunting as he fucks me just the way he said he would.

Me. Me. Me. He only wants me.

Releasing my neck, his hand digs into my hair, yanking it back. My lips part open, and my muscles ache from the position he has me in. But I don't think this is supposed to feel comfortable.

"*Fuck.* Rowan—"

"Shh, angel. Be quiet while I use your pretty hole."

He says it like this is only for him and his pleasure—as if I'm nothing but a fuck toy who only exists to serve him. The thought is what brings me to my tipping point, and I have no choice but to come with his cock still pounding hard and fast inside me.

I moan through the tears falling down my cheeks, as Rowan's cum suddenly fills me up at the same time.

It's warm and sticky, and my pussy swallows it up willingly, not letting a single drop slide back. He comes with a grunt, and I know for sure that this is a sound I'm going to remember for the rest of my life.

"You," he breathes out, repeating the one word that I know means so much. His cock exits me, and he spins me around, lifting me up only to sit me back down on the desk, this time facing him.

His mouth crashes against mine, the seam of my lips opening for him as he pushes his tongue past them. I welcome him in. My legs coil around his torso and I can feel his cum sliding out of me, but he's quick to stop it with two fingers into my pussy, pushing it back where it belongs. I'm on birth control—but he kind of makes me wish I wasn't.

"What am I doing right now?" he asks, giving my swollen lips a short break as he pins me down with his gaze.

"You're—*ahh*," I close my eyes, leaning into his touch. "Fucking my pussy. With your cum."

"*My* pussy. Not yours. It's not yours anymore, angel."

He places a kiss on my head and steps away, tucking himself back into his pants.

"Stay just like that. Don't move."

I nod and follow him around with my eyes as he goes to retrieve something from a black box on one of his shelves. He's so handsome with the morning light braiding into his features. My pussy keeps throbbing— wanting him to come back.

"It's hard to have to wait for everything I want to do to you. But when we get back to Washington—"

"Yes," I say with a hushed sound, trying to find my breathing pattern. "I'll wait. I'll wait as long as you need if you promise to do that again."

A smile. "Not so fast," he says, taking what looks like a butt plug out of an elegant cloth satchel. He prowls toward me, and I feel the need to clamp my legs together.

Not there.

He's played with my ass a little bit and it felt good, but only with his finger. That thing looks massive and there's no way it will fit inside me.

"What did I tell you? Open for me."

I don't do it immediately, and his hand reaches in between my legs, teasing my puckered hole. My pussy delights in it, but I'm still afraid.

"No need to fight it, angel. I'm going to own this too."

He pushes the plug inside my pussy first, coating it in his cum and my wetness, swirling it around until it's fully soaked. Then he takes it out and presses it to the entrance of my ass.

"It's getting in either way—if you don't want it to hurt, lie back and relax for me."

Fuck.

Carefully, I lean back on my hands and prop one knee to the side, feeling my ass and my pussy open before him.

"Very good girl," he praises, pushing the plug slowly inside. I tense up a bit but make an effort to relax through it as he watches the object enter me. "Almost there. Can you feel it?"

"Yes." I rub my lips together.

I can feel it all right.

My hole burns and stretches around the object, and my pussy betrays me by pulsing in response.

"Your ass is so tight, angel. I can't wait to feel it around my cock."

The thought of that happening sends shivers down my spine. He's huge, and I don't see how it would ever happen without splitting me in half.

"Now," he says, and I realize the whole thing went in without much pain. There's a white diamond at the end of the plug, and it makes my hole look like a treasure of sorts.

"Breakfast is on the table. I want you to go and eat everything on your plate. Then I'll take us back to my house, where I have a very special task for you to complete."

"What is it?" I ask, while part of my brain remains focused on the plug inside me. I can't not think about it the entire time. It's such a strange but pleasant sensation. I wish I didn't feel so embarrassed about it, but I think... I think I might like this more than I thought.

"I'll be gone for a few hours after we land. And every half hour, I want you to lie down in our bed and stick two fingers in that sweet pussy, fucking it slowly until you come on your hand. Will you do that for me?"

I nod, but I don't understand.

"Why are you asking me to do this when you'll be gone anyway?" I ask timidly.

"Because I can. And because I'll know you'll be doing it in my sheets this time. No longer just a distant memory I'm not allowed to touch or even think about."

He plants a kiss at the top of my head and tells me to get dressed so we can fly back.

I find myself letting him take control of everything, again and again. Bewildered by the object claiming me in my most private part, I watch him exit the room, thinking about how little I actually know about this incredible man. Other than what he's told me and what I found out from the press, I don't really know anything at all.

All I know is that there's a plug in my ass.

That his cum is leaking out on my thighs.

And that I'm supposed to watch the clock while I tease my pussy and think of him.

It's a few hours later, and I'm scrolling my phone on Rowan's veranda, back in Washington. Since it's still the weekend and my court case got ridiculously delayed, it's not like I had to be anywhere but here, at his house. Still, I tried telling him that maybe I should wait for him at *my* apartment, just because I didn't want to be excessively needy when we've just started… whatever this is between us.

But of course he saw right through me, and made me promise I wouldn't think badly about myself again. He insisted that he *wants* me to be needy and longing for him as much as he is for me. So… here I am.

Rowan's house is massive—with lush, trimmed turf surrounding it, a nearby pond, and a backyard that stretches out far longer than I could even see from when I stepped out of the car. A stark contrast from my tiny rented apartment in the suburbs of Washington.

Here, on the veranda that opens up to the garden, the smell of roses, the sun, and the warm breeze feel like silk draping over my skin. And even though he's not even here right now, I feel his presence everywhere around me. It's in the sophisticated scents floating in the air, and especially in the style of the dark, moody furniture he picked up that suits him so well.

There's a cook making lunch for me right now, despite my insistence that it wasn't necessary at all. And apparently, Saint—the man who connected me with Rowan on yesterday's call—is also working at the house, though I'm not exactly sure what he does. He seemed on edge the entire time Rowan was here before he left to deal with his meetings, which definitely struck me as strange. He's in the military too, after all.

Thankfully, right now he's made himself scarce. I don't think he likes babysitting me any more than I like him around. That's mainly because, well... I'm still wearing the plug Rowan pushed inside my ass.

I can still feel it, and every movement sends tingles inside my pussy that keep me aroused. Who knew I'd love this so much. I'm giddy at the thought of Rowan coming back to me. So, to pass the time, I'm checking in with the world for a while by scrolling on my phone. Until the clock marks another half an hour passed.

I go on social media briefly and smile at the photo carousels posted by Sterling and Lucian. They're in love, and Bali looks incredible. I'm happy for them, even more so now that I can actually experience the feeling myself.

Before I can leave them a string of enthusiastic comments, the door of a nearby car slams shut, getting my attention. Is Rowan back already?

But then I hear Saint's voice in the distance, and he does not sound happy. A woman's voice then joins him, fighting back. What the hell? They talk over each other, and I can hear them louder and louder through the house behind me.

I turn my head and catch a glimpse of a tall woman walking through the house and toward the veranda. She's dressed in a bronze maxi dress that flows gracefully on her hips, a wood-colored Hermes bag hanging from her hand. Huge curls adorn her small but chiseled head, and I almost gape at how beautiful she is.

I straighten my shoulders and force a smile.

"Hello, there," she chirps, her voice warm like chocolate. "Maybe you can tell me where Rowan is?"

"Miss Chevrier, please... you can't be here. The Commander isn't allowing—"

"Saint, for the love of God, let me at least catch my breath."

"Miss Chevrier—"

"It's okay," I say, getting up to a standing position. "I can keep Miss Chevrier company until Rowan gets back. I'm happy to, in fact."

"See? This girl has more manners than you've ever shown me. Leave us," she commands, as if she has any real power over him. I cringe at the way she treats him, but don't say anything either. Who the hell is this woman? And why does she think she can call me a "girl" when we're probably the same goddamn age?

I straighten my spine as I pin her down with my gaze. She returns it before plopping down in one of the chairs next to mine, her bag waiting for her at her perfectly manicured feet.

"Odette. Pleased to meet you," she says, dragging a

hand through her long hair. "I came looking for Rowan. Where is he?"

Odette Chevrier. I make a mental note of this name and remind myself to ask Rowan about her.

"He's at the garrison," I lie, because I don't want her to think I'm waiting for him here like a good pup. Which, admittedly, I am. "He should be back in a few hours, though last night he returned pretty late. Is there anything I can help you with instead?"

She stares back, a smirk plastered on her pouty red lips.

"He hasn't told you where he is, has he? Don't worry. He does that a lot."

My heart drums in my chest at being caught in a lie.

"I'm sorry, who are you? Why are you looking for him?"

Odette picks up a small box of cigarettes from her bag and pushes one past her lips before she takes it between her fingers to light it. Smoke wafts over in the air above her as she inhales.

"Rowan and I are fucking," she says, completely unashamed. My legs turn leaden and anxiety starts roiling in my stomach at the sound of it. I want to rip that smirk off her face. But I don't. Instead, I steady myself and sprawl across my chair, trying to look disinterested.

"When?" I ask.

She smiles, huffing the white smoke above her head.

"Whenever he wants," she shoots back, and I think she catches a glimpse of my micro expressions, because she laughs. A loud, charismatic laugh that brings men to their knees, no doubt. "What's your name?"

"Dove. And I'm sorry, but I really don't remember ever seeing you around..."

As if it hasn't been just *one* day since Rowan took me to his bed.

"Well, *Dove*, jealousy looks cute on you. Let me guess: you're his new obsession, aren't you?"

I keep silent, an involuntary scowl directed at her.

"Just Rowan being Rowan." She tilts her head, puffing out more smoke as she fixes her gold bracelet.

"Meaning?"

She shrugs. "He's a man like no other, as I'm sure you've already experienced yourself. He develops these obsessions from time to time... with certain foods or drinks, sports cars... music... and now, apparently, with random girls too." She rolls her eyes. "You're pretty— don't get me wrong. But enough to tame Rowan?" She ponders her own question, trying to figure out the answer by herself.

I cross my legs and arms, shame burning my cheeks as I listen to the words coming out of her mouth. Am I his new obsession? And if I am, how long until he gets bored of me and tosses me away?

The need to know more about Rowan crashes down on my chest again—to know him, the *real* him, not whatever the press deems newsworthy. Still, I refuse to cower before this woman, even if she is right. Because right now, Rowan's mine and I am his, and I'll be damned if I let him go without a fight.

"I've known Rowan for years. He knows my family, too. I don't know who you are and why you think you can just waltz in here and threaten me, but I assure you, he and I go way back. And he hasn't mentioned you even once. Saint!" I call out, and he storms into the garden as if he's been waiting around the corner this whole time. "Please see Miss Chevrier back to her car. I believe we've bonded enough."

Odette smacks her lips and pulls her bag into her lap.

"I'm not threatening you, Dove. But I will give you some friendly advice—if you want to drag this out for longer—don't give him everything he wants all at once."

Rage burns through me and I struggle to keep my composure. Because her words hit home. And I hate that. I hate that I don't value myself enough to think there's no way Rowan would tire of me if I gave him everything he wanted.

"Have a good day," I tell her, and Saint approaches her as she gets up.

"Likewise, birdie." She halts. "Tell Rowan to give me a call. He has yet to make good on the promise he made me last time."

Saint leads her back into the house and out the front door, while I'm left alone with my thoughts and my self-doubt. The alarm on my phone rings, and I know another half an hour is up. I'm supposed to be in Rowan's bed right now, finger-fucking myself while I think of him.

But I can't. I won't. Because what if what she said is right? What if the only way to Rowan's heart is to keep him waiting for me... to keep *him* anticipating my touch?

Flustered and disoriented, I get up from my chair and catch Saint just as he's entering the house.

"Saint, I'm sorry, but something's come up at home. Do you think you can give me a ride?"

"Christ. Why is everything working against me today? You don't understand how he'll react when he finds out you're gone—and that *I* helped you leave."

"Please, Saint. I will leave him a message myself. And I'll tell him I gave you no choice. Please?"

He sighs. "I'll get the car."

EIGHT

I flick through the files on my computer aimlessly, my stomach sending flashes of anxiety-induced pain that I can't seem to get rid of. Not even with the chamomile tea I'm sipping on, which usually helps. I try to focus on work, but my mind keeps going elsewhere. To Rowan.

It's pretty late, and he hasn't called yet.

I don't even know why I'm expecting him to do it. I left on my own volition, and maybe the message I left was convincing enough. Though I can't help but secretly wish he'd reach out. Because if he does that, then maybe... maybe what Odette said isn't true. Maybe he isn't fucking another woman at the same time while leading me to believe I'm the only one.

Fuck.

I should've stayed—should've asked him about it instead of fleeing like a scaredy-cat. But then again, if I *had* stayed, I would've made it too easy for him to just deny everything so he could fuck me again. I don't know what to do. I don't know what the hell I'm supposed to do.

I wish I could call Sterling and talk to her about it. But she's on her honeymoon... and Rowan is Commander of the Army, for God's sake! Am I even supposed to reveal this relationship or whatever the hell it is?

I. Don't. Know.

I close the lid of my laptop with a groan and pull out my phone to go on social media and numb my pain with distractions. But just as Sterling's face pops up on my feed, a knock at my door makes me jolt upright.

Nerves bundle up in my stomach, making me jittery as if I've just chugged three black coffees one after another. I bite my lip to hide my involuntary smile. But when I open the door, it is *not* the person I was expecting to see tonight. Not even fucking close.

"Hey, pup." Jared smiles with that lazy, effortless smile of his that every girl on campus used to fall for. All but me. Which is why, I'm assuming, he's still chasing me down.

"Jared..." I say with a sigh. "What are you doing here?"

We haven't been in contact much since we graduated, but he's still friends with Sterling and Lucian. Which means that when I hang out with them... he tags along too sometimes.

He shrugs. "I was in the area. Thought I'd take you out for a drink."

Sure he was.

"Well, I hate to disappoint but I'm working," I say,

crossing my arms.

He rolls his eyes and smirks.

"You're *always* working. Are you at least going to invite me in?"

I pause, considering the alternative—which is to stare at my phone for God knows how long, expecting Rowan to call.

"Fine. One drink. But then I'm going to kick you out. I've got things to do for—"

"Yeah, yeah." He walks past me inside my apartment. "Angelica Pratt. Employer of the year," he says sarcastically as I shut the door closed behind me.

I sigh and go into the kitchen, where he's leaning against the counter already waiting for me.

"What do you want? I've got Coke and..." I pick up a half-empty bottle. "Gin and tonic."

He keeps silent, and when I turn toward him, I catch him staring at me with a spark in his eyes.

"Jared..."

Not this again. Ever since that night we had sex years ago, he kept making subtle and not-so-subtle moves to get me back. Either through Sterling or just by sending me a text and ghosting me again the next hour. Why, I have no idea. But he just won't let it go.

"*Dove*," he shoots back. "I'm not the same guy I was in college. I figured my shit out. I've got a great job. I'm saving up for a house. I'm doing it—adulting like we're supposed to," he laughs. "But I still don't have *you*. Let me take you out. Let me show you how much I've changed. That night with you... Christ, I can still feel you on my skin. You were..."

"Lying there like a log?" I lift an eyebrow. "You didn't even like me that much. What the hell are you talking about?"

He rolls his eyes and closes the space between us, placing his hands on my shoulders.

"I was an idiot back then. That's what I'm saying—I've changed. If you would just... let me show you."

I don't want him. I know I don't. But I'm hurting. And Rowan hasn't called, and maybe going out for a walk doesn't sound that bad.

"You're considering it," he smiles, touching his forehead to mine.

I don't like the gesture—it feels wrong, and I want to push him away.

"I..."

My ringing phone gives me an opportunity to step away without making this even more awkward than it already is. I clear my throat and turn on my heels as I rush to pick it up. I can hear Jared slowly following behind. An unknown number pops up, and my pulse starts racing against my skin.

I'm itching to answer. But not now. Not when Jared is here.

"Listen, Jared. I really need you to leave. I can't do this right now."

"Dove..."

I head back into the hallway, this time to open the front door for him.

"You were considering it," he says as he follows me. "Why not give this a chance? Give *us* a chance?"

"I'm not exactly... available right now," I say,

wrapping my hand around the doorknob.

"That's bullshit. I asked Sterling and she told me—"

"You asked Sterling?!" I look back at him, annoyance surging in my tone.

I open the door at the same time. And both Jared and I stop talking.

Shock spreads on my face when I see the silhouette of Commander Rowan King staring back at us, completely dominating the space. He looks taller. He looks upset. And he looks unforgiving.

I gulp, making a mess of my breathing pattern but trying to keep it under control.

Why the hell is Rowan here? *How* can he be here?

"Hello, angel." His low voice tingles my senses. It's an effort of stubborn will not to lean into it.

"What the hell?" Jared frowns, stepping in front of me and doing his best to take control of the situation. "I'm Jared Carter. What is—"

"A pleasure to meet you, Jared. Am I interrupting?" Rowan asks, looking at me. Only looking at me.

I hold my breath, not knowing what to say or do. I'm shaking. And for once, I'm glad Jared can actually talk for both of us. Because I'm equally as stunned as he is right now.

It's one thing to meet Rowan in his environment,

where everything is new and operating by his rules. And it's another to see him here, in my small apartment, where he's like a bull in a china shop.

"Well, I'm sure your visit is way more important than whatever we were doing, sir. How can we—"

"Dove?" Rowan asks again, and I don't fail to notice his subtle frown at the idea that Jared and I were doing something.

"I... um... Jared." I touch his shoulder, getting his attention. "Please... I'll call you tomorrow."

But he isn't moving.

"The hell you will. I'm not leaving you alone. I'm here for you," he says, as if this is something he can protect me from. He can't. No one can—except maybe my stupid little safe word. But right now I'm not even sure that would work anymore.

I look at Rowan, catching his gaze. The way he stares into my soul sends literal shivers down my spine. His eyes are burning with a mix of feelings I can't decipher right now on my own. So I avert them like a coward, and focus back on Jared. I open my mouth once more to convince him to leave, but Rowan beats me to it.

"Dove and I have something important to discuss. Her brother worked under my command, as you probably know."

"Oh, shit," he says, looking back at me. "Well, yeah. That makes sense, I guess. Will you—"

"Yes. I'll call," I insist. "Have a good night."

Rowan steps to the side, and Jared walks past him, making the contrast between them even more stark. At 27, Jared still looks like a boy compared to Rowan, whose training and strict routines have chiseled him into a masculine, imposing, and dominant man despite only being a few years older. I gulp at the sight and watch as Jared walks down the hall, stealing one more glance our way.

Rowan steps into my tiny apartment, slowly and controlled like a panther scouting new hunting grounds.

"Can I get you anything—" I blurt out, but he cuts me off.

"*Something's come up. Saint had no choice but to drive me back. Sorry!*" Rowan recites the message I left on his dining table before I left his house. "And then I walk in here and find you all flustered with another man's scent all over you. Things aren't looking too good for you right now, angel. Explain," he orders.

I take in a huge lungful of air, dragging a hand through my hair.

"Jared is an old friend. It wasn't... it wasn't like that."

"It wasn't like that?" he muses, dipping his chin, his eyes darkening. "Then why is my property reeking of some cheap perfume that was clearly picked to lure you into a fuck session tonight?"

His nostrils flare, and his jaw clenches, but he doesn't take a step toward me. It's almost as if he wants me to move toward him first. But I can't—not until we settle whatever conversation Odette and I had.

"Okay, first of all," I say, making an effort to look into his eyes. "I'm not your property. You don't get to call me that when you've been fucking other women behind my back. Jared is an old friend—and he might've tried to get me to go out with him tonight. But I wasn't interested. Even though maybe I *should* have gone. Because if what Odette Chevrier said is true, then—"

"Dove. I am not fucking anyone else but you," he deadpans. "I don't *want* anyone else but you."

"Well..." I trail off, my argument now holding no weight. "Well then why did she say otherwise?"

"We fucked twice. It was years ago. And in the same night. She was just a means to an end."

"A means to an end?"

"Yes. Her father is a congressman. We needed funds for a certain mission, and we knew he was going to vote against it. Odette said she could sway him, so... we each got what we wanted that night. Period."

Jesus Christ. All the years of therapy after my father left and I still can't think through this straight. All I know is that if Rowan ever tells me there's someone else—I'm done. No matter how much I want him, I can't let myself fall into the same trap my mother did. Tears swarm at the backs of my eyes, but I don't let them fall. I swallow them back instead.

"Okay," I look down at my feet. "But clearly, she doesn't think that was the end of it. She still wants you."

"And she can continue to want me, for all I care. You are mine as much as I am yours, angel. Things are really fucking clear to me. And if you can't see that yet, I'm going to make sure you do."

I guess... I guess I can't argue with that.

I let loose a soft but shaky breath and watch as he finally closes the distance between us. He lifts my chin up with his index finger and I'm forced to look back into his eyes.

"So you lied to me then," he smiles. "Nothing's come up, has it, angel? You just heard what you wanted to hear... and you ran from me like a scared pup. Is that it?"

"I'm sorry," I whisper. "That was stupid of me. But what would *you* do if some sexy-looking dude came to you and told you he's been fucking me behind your back?"

"Easy. I'd cut off his cock. Make him eat it. And tie him up to a pole so he can watch while I make you come on my tongue."

I stifle a laugh but it falters when I see he's not joking.

"Dove. You were right to run away for one reason only—I am not a good man. I've done things that if you knew about you'd never want to see me again. Which is why I'm always going to give you a choice. You can leave me anytime you want. You're not bound to me, not as bound as I am to you. All I ask is that before you decide to rip my heart open, you warn me about it first. You tell me what's on your mind... and we talk about it. And then... then you can leave me behind if that's what's best for you. I will never—"

"Stop. Rowan, stop. I want you so much I don't know what to do with this feeling. I'm not going to leave. You don't scare me. I just wish..."

"Yes?"

"I just wish I got to know you a little bit more. I want all of you, not just scraps."

He smiles, his hand coiling around my neck possessively, but without squeezing it.

"Good. I also want to know you. Which is why I'm taking you out tonight."

NINE

I walk back out into the living room wearing my silky cerulean dress that I bought for Sterling's wedding this summer. I argued that I'd look out of place in it while eating at a restaurant, but Rowan insisted the place he is taking me to understands no such thing as being overdressed. So I indulged him.

I coat my lips with a layer of gloss. Approaching him, his eyes roam across my body as he listens to someone talking to him over the phone. I don't know what he's thinking—his expression doesn't offer much.

He crooks a finger in my direction, demanding me to come closer. And when I do, his hand slips through the slit of the fabric that's covering my legs, trailing up until it reaches my panties. He hooks his finger behind the thin material and pulls it down until it slides off easily from the rest of my thighs and I'm naked underneath my dress.

"Rowan—" I whisper, though I'm not really sure what I'm asking. I missed him all day.

"Just one moment, please, Mr. President," he says into the phone, and my eyes widen in shock.

It can't be. Rowan's messing with me—he can't possibly be talking to the President of the United States of America right now. Not when his fingers are so close to my pussy and his eyes are devouring me from afar.

But the more I stare at him with my breath held tight in my lungs, the more I realize there's no trace of pretense in his demeanor. Of course there isn't. Rowan isn't the kind of man who hides who he is and what he does—even if the things he does might seem crazy to the rest of us.

This man, he's so... unpredictable. So unapologetic in everything he does. It's in this moment that I realize just how addictive being around him is. Suddenly, it's not just my body longing for him anymore. No. It feels like my heart is slipping through the cracks of my ribcage, wanting to give itself fully over to him.

Lowering the phone to his side, Rowan catches my gaze and I snap out of my thoughts, feeling my cheeks flush and nervousness inundate my veins.

"Leave the panties at home," he says. "I'm going to have full access to your gorgeous pussy tonight. Is that understood?"

I nod softly, my mind going back to the person waiting for him on the other end of the line.

"Is that... Are you really talking to the president right now?" I whisper.

He only smirks at me, and that is answer enough.

"I want you to get down on your hands and knees. Ass facing me." He dips his chin toward the floor, indicating the place where he wants me.

"But—"

"Now, angel."

Fuck. Okay, I guess. It's not like *I'm* the one talking to the president, after all. I press my lips together and bite down on my inner cheek, lowering myself to the floor in front of him.

"Good girl," he says, and when he sees that I'm taking the position he requested, he finally resumes his conversation.

My pussy tingles with excitement at being praised, but I still can't fathom what's going on. How can he be so calm... so collected? As if the president is nothing but an old friend he banters with from time to time. I don't even know. Maybe he *is* one. I remind myself, once again, that I don't know much about Rowan's life.

I breathe in and out, looking straight ahead, with my ass pointing toward him. I don't know what he wants to do, but I'm glad I didn't take out that butt plug. Somehow, I was hoping he'd call... that he'd tell me there's nothing going on between him and Odette. So I kept it there just in case.

Rowan's hand lifts up my dress, revealing me to him. I gasp when he pushes the plug in further, but my body sags when he pulls it out completely. I feel empty now, and I'm not sure I like it. When I turn to look at what he's doing, I'm met with a stern look that has me looking back toward the floor in an instant. I whimper, waiting for whatever he wants to do to me.

Cold liquid drips down on my hole and I jolt upright at the surprise sensation. A palm lands on my ass, pain spreading across it, and I understand he wants me to be silent. But it's hard—it's really fucking hard when another, much bigger plug pushes at the entrance of my hole, wanting to fill me up again. I press a hand to my mouth to stifle my moans, though I'm not sure how much it helps.

"Rock your body back and forth," Rowan says, and I presume he's put his microphone on mute for a second there.

I nod and do as I'm told, the plug entering my tight ass inch by inch whenever I push myself into it. It hurts, but not as much as the first one did. So I brace myself and take it all the way in, my body finally relaxing under the tingles of arousal pulsing through my core.

A finger then slides inside my pussy and it just stays there, unmoving. I take it as a sign to rock my body into Rowan's touch again, but when I do he removes it and slaps my ass. He slides it back in and this time, when I don't move, he keeps it there.

I can feel my pussy getting wetter and wetter by the second. There's something oddly erotic about being wrapped around his finger like that, even if he's not fucking me. Still, I want more. I want him to make me come. So I look back at him with pleading eyes, hoping he'll indulge me this time.

"Of course. Send all my best to the First Lady. Yes, hopefully soon. Good night."

I hear the phone being tossed away on the couch, and I know the call has ended.

"Is there a problem, angel?"

"N-No, sir."

"Liar, liar, pants on fire," he purrs and caresses my ass with his free hand.

"I just... it feels good. But..."

"But you would very much like to be finger-fucked?"

"Yes," I gasp, closing my eyes and rocking myself into his touch.

Smack.

"What did I tell you this morning? You'll stay still and take what I'm giving you. I could keep my finger inside your wet pussy all night long without moving it and you wouldn't be able to do anything about it. Do you understand that?"

"Yes, sir."

He offers a hum of approval at the same time as my pussy clenches around his finger, begging him to stop teasing me. But when he finally moves it, he slides it out of me completely, drawing a frown and a few small tears of frustration out of me.

Damn him for punishing me like this. Though I can't say I don't deserve it after running from him today.

"Don't cry, angel. When we get back, I'll fuck your little ass over this desk right here. And then I'll take a few long hours making this pussy come until you beg me to stop."

My heels make contact with the pavement as I take Rowan's hand and let him gently pull me out of the car. I've never held his hand before. It feels warm and rough on the edges, and it spurs all sorts of fuzzy feelings inside me. I look up at him through my eyelashes, the sight of him under the moonlight making my heart skip a beat.

Hooded dark green eyes stare back at me, owning me and giving themselves over to me at the same time. His lush lips twist into a subtle smile. I return it, and for a long moment I zone out of everything else around us, seeing him and him only.

He's so goddamn handsome. And he's mine.

"Who do you belong to, Dove?" he asks, interlacing his fingers with mine.

I waste no seconds to tell him the truth.

"You. I belong to you."

"Don't you dare forget that. We're about to meet a lot of people, and I want to make sure they all know what you just told me."

"W-Who are we meeting?"

He pulls my slight hand to his lips and imprints himself on me with a kiss before leading us to the entrance of what looks like another fancy hotel. I walk beside him with my long dress wafting around my legs, making it look as if I'm walking on a moving cloud.

A woman comes out before us, immediately recognizing Rowan. She smiles at him in a way that makes my blood boil while completely overlooking me. My hand tenses in Rowan's grasp, and he tilts his head toward me as we follow her through the hotel.

"Her name is Vanda," he whispers, "and all the wives

you're about to meet hate her with a near-homicidal passion."

I purse my lips to hide my laugh.

"Did she..." I whisper back.

"Oh, yeah. Slept with nearly all the senators and government agents you're about to meet tonight."

I open my mouth to say something, but just then, Vanda stops in front of two large doors and extends her hand forward as she keeps fluttering her eyelashes at Rowan. I can hear the tune of a classical song from the room beyond, but nothing more.

"Thank you," Rowan says without sparing her another glance.

Opening one of the doors, he leads us both inside, and all eyes are on us. Not all of them are happy, which makes me feel even more nervous than I thought I'd have to be.

My pulse hikes up to my throat, but Rowan's thumb swipes across the back of my hand, reminding me that he's got me. All I need to do is let him take care of me. Of us.

I'm led toward a large table where men and women wearing suits and dresses talk about God-knows-what. I don't recognize anyone, though it doesn't surprise me. Other than watching Rowan on TV before he reached out, I've never really followed politics.

A middle-aged man approaches us, grinning as he looks between me and Rowan. A woman follows close behind him, until they both stop in front of us.

"I've lived to see the day Rowan King brought a woman to our parties," the man says. The woman—his wife, I presume—sips on champagne while looking me up and down.

"Senator Gutenberg." Rowan dips his head, acknowledging his presence. "Mrs. Gutenberg."

"An outsider, too," Mrs. Gutenberg muses. Her tone indicates she's satisfied by the fact.

"This is Dove Finnegan," Rowan says, letting go of my hand only to snake his arm around my waist, pulling me closer to him possessively. "And yes, she's mine."

The way he says it makes my cheeks flush, especially when I'm reminded of the plug he pushed inside my ass. Rowan's promise of fucking it when we get back has me pressing my legs together in anticipation.

"A pleasure to meet you," I chirp, but it comes out quieter than I would like.

"Finnegan?" the senator asks, both his eyebrows lifting at the same time. "She's related to Cole?"

"Oh, honey, I'm sorry for your loss," his wife says, leaning in to grab my hand.

So they knew my brother, then.

"Thank you," I say, forcing a smile.

The senator tsks, looking back at Rowan. "And you're not worried they're going to target her?"

There's a short pause that has me looking back at him, too, for answers. Target who? Me? Who is he talking about? Rowan tightens his grip on me, and I get the feeling something's not right.

"Like I said," he drawls, "she's mine. So other than making sure I'm giving her a perfect evening, I'm not worried about anything else. Now, if you'll excuse us—"

Rowan takes my hand and leads me around the senator and his wife. But just as I'm about to pass them, Mrs. Gutenberg catches my other hand and stops me in my tracks for a brief second.

"Be careful, Dove Finnegan. Or you might not get out of this alive."

TEN

I push my lower lip between my teeth, tasting the red wine I've just sipped. It goes down with a subtle burn, mixing with the nerves swarming in my belly. Rowan is across the small rounded table, watching me, waiting for me to answer the question he has just asked.

We're dating, he said. And I would love nothing more than to just give in to him tonight, but my mind keeps going back to the warning Mrs. Gutenberg issued to me. What did she mean by that? And why is Rowan so clearly avoiding the subject?

"I like giving people a voice," I finally say, placing my glass back on the table. "People who don't have one, I mean. That's why I wanted to become a lawyer."

It's not the full truth, but I don't know how much of my sob story Rowan wants to hear. I'm sure he'd much rather enjoy himself at this party. So I decide against telling him about my cheating father and the way he blackmailed me and my brother for years before finally leaving our mom.

Silence passes between us, and Rowan cocks his head slightly to the right, observing me.

"I find it really interesting how easily I can read you, angel. I wish you'd trust me with your past, but in truth, I haven't given you much to trust yet. You're right to be cautious, though I promise you have nothing to worry about."

My lips part lightly, liking the way he pays attention to me. It's not that I don't trust him. For some reason, I have blind faith in this man. I'd do anything he asked knowing he'd never hurt me. Stupid? Maybe. But I can't help it. Whatever heartbreak Rowan might cause me in the future, I know it would be all worth it.

"I just didn't want to bore you with the details," I say as I wave a hand in front of me.

"Bore me?" He scoffs. "I want to know everything about you, Dove. Your favorite flowers. Your earliest memory. Whether you prefer watching the sun rise or set. Your favorite color too while we're at it. You've lived in my head for too long. And now I finally get to have you. So let me have you."

My gaping turns into smirking, and placidness starts coursing through me, replacing my nerves. "My favorite color?" I muse. "Sounds easy enough. And here I was thinking you'd want to know my favorite kink or something crazy like that."

He smiles, his eyes never leaving mine, the silence drifting between us making me understand he really does want an answer to those questions.

I fix my bracelet and clear my throat, averting his

persistent gaze as I try to find my words.

"I like peonies the most—white and pink. My earliest memory is playing hide-and-seek with Cole between the white sheets my mother had left outside to dry. Sunrises scare me, because only bad things happen when you're up at the early hours of dawn, so I prefer sunsets. And my favorite color?" I grin, then look back at the green in his eyes. "Right now, green. Your turn."

He leans back in his chair, his lips twitching with a smile.

"What would you like to know?"

"Everything you can tell me," I say. "Why did you join the military, for one? And how are you so"—I shake my head lightly—"calm, considering what's going on in the country? You're a real mystery to me."

He doesn't answer immediately. Instead, I gasp when Rowan pulls me and my chair closer to him with a screech as it slides across the polished floors. Then I feel the warmth of his palm trailing up the slit in my dress.

"Rowan!" I whisper-shout, looking around for anyone who might see us.

"I ought to be a gentleman and get through this dinner without touching you. But that perfume of yours is driving me insane. You smell delicious."

I'm lost for words as he takes the breath out of my lungs again. I stare at his lush lips, and all I want to do is press mine to his.

"Is it truly okay if people see us together? For politics, I mean."

His other hand cups my small face and brings me

closer to his, until we're mere inches apart. I can feel his warm breath tickling my skin.

"Are you still feeling the plug in your pretty hole, angel?"

"Yes," I say, now centering my attention on it even more.

"Good. Stay still while I check to see how wet you are. I want everyone to know you're mine, but I don't want them to see what I do to you. So don't move. Understand?"

I nod, feeling his fingers trail higher on my leg until they reach my naked pussy lips. This is why he didn't want me wearing underwear tonight. My breath catches in my throat as I'm trying to fight the flush taking over my cheeks.

The tip of Rowan's middle finger dips deeper in between my folds, a whimper escaping me in response. He's still holding my gaze as his hand explores my pussy, and it's intimate in ways I've never experienced before. I'm not just wet, I'm drenched. And butterflies come to life in my belly knowing it'll please him.

"Commander Rowan King." A male voice startles me from somewhere in front of us. Thank God we're hiding what we're doing behind the table.

I turn my face toward him and notice he's got a camera in his hands.

"Mind if I take your picture? You look lovely together, and America would love to see who stole our commander's heart."

"Rowan..." I plead, shame washing over me knowing his hand is still all over my pussy while this man is talking to us.

"Just one moment, Alistar," Rowan says to the guy, then turns to speak to me without him hearing. "I'd actually like you to remember this moment. I want you to see yourself in the papers tomorrow and know your pussy was at my mercy under this table while you posed for a picture like the pretty girl you are. I want you to remember you're mine, and no one else's. But if you'd rather keep us a secret for a while, I understand. This would plaster your face all over the country, and if you're not comfortable with that, I'll tell him to fuck off. So tell me what you want, angel."

His fingers pinch my clit under the table, and I bite my lip to stifle a moan.

I part my legs a few inches, and he slides inside me with one finger, pumping it lightly so that his muscles don't clench too much and give us away. I'm so turned on right now I can't believe what he wants us to do.

But fuck it, I want to remember this just as much as he does. Besides, I don't want to be just a little secret he's hiding from the world. I want to be his everything, and I want the world to know that he's mine.

"I want you," I say honestly, and he smiles, curling his finger upward to touch my G-spot. I wrap my fingers around his thigh, squeezing it to stop myself from coming undone right here and now.

"Then smile at the camera, angel. Show the world that you're mine."

And so I do. Alistar grins, too, probably excited he's going to be the first photographer to sell an image of us, and starts taking a few rapid shots.

"Beautiful," he says, then turns to leave with a short nod. "Enjoy your evening."

Rowan retracts his fingers from my pussy at the same time, and I clench my thighs together to keep adding some friction.

"You're drenched, angel. I love seeing how much that plug gets you worked up."

"Please...?"

He smiles, placing a kiss on my lips instead of giving my pussy the release it so desperately wants. "When we get home, that's all I'm going to do. Play with your pink pussy until you beg me to stop. Here, they'll see your pretty face when you come, and I'd rather keep that image all to myself. Now, where were we?"

I clear my throat, trying my hardest not to look flustered about being teased so much.

"You didn't answer my question. About joining the military."

He nods, suddenly taking on a serious look. "My father served the country. So did my grandfather. I was pushed toward it from an early age, and didn't feel like I had a say in it."

I've done enough therapy to understand this is probably why he feels the need to control everything around him now that he can. I'd like to know more, but I won't push too much on this. Not yet.

"Did you want to do something else?"

"I never even considered another path. My mother wanted me to run for office instead—thought I'd be better off that way. But I never wanted that much power. I was worried of what I might do with it."

Kill them all, I recall him saying this morning when talking to Sergeant Rhames. I didn't even think much about it, considering Rowan's job. I wonder if I should.

"Then I met Cole," he says, and a sad smile spreads on his lips. "I also met Maddox Thorne, the president, and they became like family to me. It's why I stayed in the military. Why I climbed my way up to the top. The three of us were going to run the country. Maddox as the president, me as the Army Commander, and Cole..." he sighs, "he was supposed to run the FBI. This country is so corrupt... so vile that we took it upon ourselves to do something about it. We thought we could, so we set things in motion between us. But then they found us out... and Cole was the first to go down because we weren't careful enough."

"W-What do you mean? Cole died on the battlefield..." I frown, taken aback by the new information. Cole was going to run the FBI? All my parents and I knew was that he was a lieutenant fighting for his country.

"It's complicated," he says. "And I'd hate to make you relive the memory of his death right now..."

"No. Please, Rowan, you have to tell me. He is— was—my brother. I need to know."

He nods once, his face suddenly becoming solemn.

"We were going up in ranks. Fast. The three of us took more risks than anyone else, and the papers kept writing about us. This is why they started noticing us— the master puppeteers pulling the real strings in the government. They saw through our plans of stealing the reins, and went after Cole first because... his death was the easiest one to cover up at the time. He was not supposed to die that night. It was a setup."

I blink away tears, but I'm more shocked than sad right now. Enraged. My brother was murdered in cold blood, and the whole country lied about it. Lied to me and his family.

"Where," I gulp, "where are these people you speak of? Why weren't they punished for this crime?"

"They were," he deadpans, before looking into my eyes. "I killed them all before Cole's body was even sent back home."

I'm sitting on my bed, still wearing the cerulean dress after Rowan brought me back from the party. He's in the bathroom, filling my tub with water. And I don't know what's worse: knowing the man I'm in love with murders people in cold blood for a living... which goes against everything I believe in, or being so accepting of the fact.

It's sick and it's twisted, but if those men really killed my brother... I can't help but secretly thank Rowan for what he did. Then again... I call myself a lawyer. Someone who believes in the justice system, who wants to give everyone a voice to defend themselves. Maybe not everyone deserves it. But who am I to decide who does and who doesn't? Who are any of us?

A rough hand caresses the side of my face, and I look

up at Rowan with tears in my eyes.

"Say something, angel. You've been quiet ever since I told you."

I lean into his touch, but shake my head against it too.

"I don't know what to say. I need to process this."

I hate this. I hate that instead of coming home and being fucked until the hours of dawn, I'm hiding from Rowan in my own head. He doesn't deserve it, yet it's the only response I can muster right now.

He goes behind me and my skin warms up where he touches it to unzip my dress. I let him do it, and even help him get me out of it until I'm naked in my bed.

"Come on," he says, extending a hand forward to take mine. "Let's get you warm and comfortable."

"Are you going back home tonight?"

Please say no. Please say no.

"I'm not going anywhere. Not unless you want me to."

A sigh of relief escapes me, and I take his hand, the feeling of him instantly bringing me back to the present moment. I let him guide me to the bathroom and I step into the warm water, my thighs clenching every time the plug in my ass reminds me it's there.

Rowan sits on the side of the tub, still fully dressed as he unbuttons only the top of his shirt.

"I'm sorry," I say, rubbing my eyes to get rid of the tears. "It's just... he was so young. And then you... you killed those people. I'm supposed to bring justice with my job, and yet..." I catch his now-soft gaze. "And yet, I'm glad you did it. What does this say about me,

Rowan?"

"That you're human," he smiles. "Things aren't so black-and-white, angel. Those people would've never stepped foot in a courtroom. They owned the courtrooms. Killing them was the only way to avenge Cole."

"Does Senator Gutenberg know about all of this?"

"Yes. He and his wife helped us with some stuff."

"Is that why she told me to be careful? Because you... kill people?"

He snorts, then pushes a lock of my hair behind my ear. "No, I wish that was it. I killed the ones who were directly responsible, but their organization has deep roots—they call themselves the Echelons of the Free World. We've yet to get to the bottom of it. Which is why I wanted to ask you something."

"What is it?" I suck in a breath, the warm water swashing against my breasts from the movement.

"Being together... is not going to be easy. The war is still not fully over. And the EFW are always plotting to take us down. It's not just the president and I that are targets. They'll use anything and anyone they can to get what they want. But now they'll see you're under my protection, which is part of why I wanted us to take that picture tonight. I don't want to scare you, I just..." He drags a hand down his face.

"I hope this isn't you trying to break up with me," I joke, but it only makes him frown deeper.

"This is me trying to get you to move in with me."

"Oh."

"You don't have to decide right now. But the sooner

you do, the better. I'd sleep much better at night knowing you're in my arms, where I can protect you."

The thought of being with him all the time makes my heart flutter. I want to, of course I want to. But the truth is, we've only been seeing each other for a few days. And I can't help but wonder if we're rushing into this.

"I'd love to, Rowan..."

"But?"

"But maybe we should wait a little bit longer. You know, to make sure this is what we really want."

I say it like that, but I hate the words coming out of my mouth. What I really wanted to say was *I don't want you to get bored of me so quickly*.

"I am absolutely certain this is what I want," he says, caressing my breast with his knuckles as if lost in thought. It gets hard, wanting more of his touch. "It's okay, angel. I'll wait until you're ready. But you'll have to let me place some of my men around your apartment to watch over you when we're not together. This isn't negotiable."

I can't say I love the idea, but I'd lie if I said Mrs. Gutenberg's warning hasn't gotten to me. Better safe than sorry, I guess.

"Sure. That would be okay. Thank you, sir," I smirk, knowing the effect that word has on him.

"Good girl. Feeling better?" New promises linger in that low voice, sending tingles down into my core.

I nod fast, knowing exactly what he plans on doing to me for the rest of the night.

ELEVEN

The early rays of dawn are breaking through the windows, casting a silent glow over my bedroom. I wake up feeling Rowan's hand between my legs, drawing soft and absent circles around my clit as if it's become his new favorite habit. My body reacts with a hushed moan, and his naked chest rumbles with sound against my back.

"One of these days, I won't be able to stop myself from using your pretty hole while you're asleep," he says in a rough morning voice. "When it comes to you, I'm a weak man. I have no self-control."

The image does something to me—something I should be afraid of. Because being used by a powerful man while you're unconscious shouldn't make your pussy wet. It shouldn't, and yet... I'm arching my ass into his already hard erection, chasing it. It's almost funny how my mind keeps trying to justify all of this, when I know full well belonging to him feels just as natural as breathing air.

"Good morning to you too," I tease, just as he slides the tip of his finger inside my slick pussy. It goes in easily, the arousal pooling at my entrance making a wet sticking sound when he smears it around.

I fell asleep coming with his name on my lips last night. I took his fingers and his tongue for as long as I could, but at some point my body shut down. Even then, he didn't stop making my legs twitch and my pussy numb from drawing orgasm after orgasm out of me. I had to beg, *beg* him to stop making me come, tears in my eyes and all. I've never in my life experienced something as exhilarating—and I loved every second of it.

"What's the time? Do you have to leave?" I try to get up on my elbow, not wanting to be too needy or make him feel like I'm keeping him from doing his job.

A strong hand wraps around my hair, tugging me back into him.

"I do," he sighs. "But not before I leave you with something to remind you of me. Come here."

He pulls my hips into his lap, and I clutch the sheets in front of me, not knowing what to expect.

Pulling the covers off to reveal my naked ass, his hand squeezes and tugs at my soft skin until I feel him getting harder under my weight. He didn't fuck my ass last night. I don't know why, and it almost made me want to ask him because I was looking forward to it. But now he's right there, swirling the plug out of me, making me feel empty and aroused.

"What are you going to do?"

"Don't ask questions you already know the answer

to," he tsks, two of his fingers replacing the plug as he pushes them inside my hole. I tense around the intrusion—it doesn't hurt yet, but I've never done this before. I'm nervous. "If you do that, it will hurt. A lot. So let me in, angel."

I nod, my breathing fractured as I let him claim this new part of me. He's caressing my hair with his free hand and I close my eyes, focusing on the buzzing sensation breaking free all throughout my body.

"Open for me," he says, lowering his hand from my hair to my lips, where two of his fingers are waiting. I do as he says, and he pushes them deep inside my mouth where my tongue can't help but start swirling around them. "So many parts of you I haven't claimed yet. I keep wanting to take my time with you, but it isn't easy. I want all of you."

I can only moan in response, with his fingers thrusting both in my mouth and in my ass, playing me like a complex instrument.

"You're going to feel so tight around my cock, angel. I won't be able to think of anything else for days. Look what you're doing to me," he muses. I don't *want* him to think about anything else.

His fingers leave my mouth, and he drags me by my hair to a sitting position, even with his fingers still in my ass. They go in even deeper now. I whimper, feeling every curve of his knuckles deep inside.

"Don't move unless I move you. Understand?"

"I understand," I gulp, my heartbeat now in a chaotic race to nowhere.

He gets out of bed first, then pulls me along. I have

no choice but to follow, since he won't remove his fingers from my hole. With his free hand, he opens my nightstand and takes the lube I bought not even two weeks ago.

"How did you know I had that?" My cheeks burn with shame.

But he doesn't answer. Instead, he pulls me along as he approaches the desk across the room, where he promised he'd bend me over.

He's going to fuck my ass. Just like he said he would.

"Rowan," I plead, fear suddenly creeping in. It's going to hurt, no matter what I do or don't do.

"I'm not going to stop, angel. Once I get inside you, there's only one thing that can make me stop fucking your pretty asshole. Do you know what it is?"

I nod quickly, feeling his palm press against my upper back, bending me over the cold desk where I do my work.

"My safe word."

"That's right. Don't ask me to stop. Don't call out my name. Neither of those things will save you. Only your safe word will. Understand?"

"Y-Yes."

The twist of a cap breaks through the silence, and the next thing I feel is the cold lube pouring down on my ass and pussy from behind. I shudder, then feel Rowan's warm hand smearing it around when he removes his fingers.

He throws the lube somewhere on the table, then uses both hands to open my thighs apart.

"Such a good girl for me. I wish you could see how

pretty you are right now, spread out and waiting for my cock in your ass."

My pussy tingles at his words, though I'm so embarrassed I wish I could disappear into thin air. I bet he sees every crevice and imperfection of my body. He can't mean that—I'm anything *but* pretty right now.

His cock inches closer and closer, until I feel him push himself inside my tight hole with just the crown. A burning sensation draws painful whimpers out of me. He's too big. He's too big, and I can't possibly take him.

"You can," he tells me, his voice low and controlled. "Relax for me. You can take it."

My muscles clench and then loosen up. He pushes farther, inch by inch, while tears start running down my cheeks. I have my safe word ready, right on the edge of my lips, but I don't say it yet. My body shakes with silent sobs.

"It hurts. It hurts so bad, Rowan."

"I know, angel. Breathe for me. You're doing so well."

I try to do what he says, but it's hard to focus on anything other than the pain. Until Rowan brings a hand between my legs, putting pressure on my clit. I mumble inaudible words, my ass suddenly clenching around him.

"That's it. Fuck, you're so tight. Just a little bit farther."

I whimper-moan when he pushes himself one last time into me, and then I feel his fingers dig into my hips. Without any warning, Rowan lifts me up and moves my upper body a bit to the right, lowering my pussy on the corner of the desk.

"Oh my God," I cry out, my clit throbbing with pleasure as the cold wood applies just the right amount of pressure on it.

"I want to watch you rub your little pussy against this desk. Can you do that for me, angel?"

He doesn't have to ask me twice. I start rubbing myself against the cold material, rocking my hips back and forth, which makes Rowan's cock thrust in and out of my ass at the same time. I do it slowly, so that I don't hurt myself. It's like being plugged into a machine only I can control.

The corner becomes slippery from my arousal coating it, my folds opened wide to let my clit slide up and down. My pussy clenches, and my ass does the same thing—only there's Rowan's hard erection to clench around.

I tilt my head backward, my mouth hanging open and my eyes closed shut. Rowan murmurs something into my ear, but I can't hear it. I'm lost in this feeling of being filled by him in a place no one has ever touched me. And I keep chasing it, squeezing every last drop of pleasure until my hips stop moving on their own accord.

A grunt ripples from Rowan's chest and he wraps his fist around my hair, tugging my head toward him as he starts fucking my ass the way he needs to. It's hard and relentless, the pain mixing with the ghost of my orgasm, making me cry out.

Just when I don't think I can take him anymore,

Rowan bites down on my shoulder, replacing the pain with another. It's going to leave a mark.

"So. Fucking. Perfect," he breathes out, consumed by chasing his own release. My hands reach out to my sides, wanting to grip something so I can steady myself. But the only thing I can touch are the sides of the desk, which isn't bringing much stability.

Thud. Thud. Thud.

The desk bangs against the wall while he fucks me, and all I can do is hold on for dear life. My eyelashes flutter closed, and I'm feeling dizzy all of a sudden. I know this feeling. My body is shutting down again. But right before I get to voice my safe word, Rowan stops, and warm sticky fluid fills my ass as he tugs my hair until I'm crashing against his hard chest.

I watch Rowan sip on a cup of black coffee with a hand in the pocket of his suit. He's all dressed and ready to leave. And I'm not thrilled about it. I wish I'd said yes to moving in with him. I don't know when I'm going to see him again.

"Come here," he rasps, and my body instantly moves into his. His tongue pushes against the seam of my lips, opening me up. He tastes like coffee and my ginger-mint toothpaste, and I smile into the kiss. "I'm going to miss you, angel. I don't know when I can see you again, but any chance I get, I'll take it. My schedule is a bit crazy right now."

"Don't worry," I say, biting my lip. "I understand. Besides, I need to work too."

He nods, placing another kiss on the top of my head before retrieving something from his chest pocket.

"Come over whenever you want. Even if I'm not there," he says, opening up my palm to place a key in it. "Security will let you in, no matter the hour."

"But if you're not there..."

"I'll know you visited. It won't be enough, but at least it's something."

"Right," I smile. He smiles back.

"I'll see you soon, angel."

And with that, the warmth of his body leaves mine, and I'm annoyed at myself for how fucking needy I feel. We've both got lives we need to get back to, after all. I hear the door opening and closing behind him, leaving me all alone in my apartment with nothing but his scent all over me and his cum still leaking out of my sore ass.

Slowly, I unfreeze myself from the spot where he was holding me, and I head into the shower to get ready for the day. At six in the morning, it's usually too early to get to the office. But Miss Pratt is already there today. And she's texted me saying that, apparently, something's gone wrong with the case and we need to dig into more files.

I lather my hair with shampoo, rinse it out, and put some makeup on once I'm dry. Then I slide into a pair of high-waisted black pants and throw on a cream shirt. By the time I'm ready to leave, it's six forty-five—still pretty early. Which is why I did *not* expect to see what I'm seeing right now in front of my apartment complex.

I open the door and dozens of photographers and journalists point their cameras and mics at me. Flashes go off, blinding me, and people talk all over each other, all wanting something from me.

What. The. Fuck.

"What's it like dating Commander Rowan King?" someone asks.

"I..."

"Does he feel responsible for Cole Finnegan's death?" someone else asks, making me frown.

"He..."

"Dove! Over here!" A woman gets my attention. "Is it true that the CCSI's attacks are more serious than what we've been led to believe?"

My phone vibrates in my purse, but I don't dare take it out to look at it. I feel violated just having these people stand in front of me. In front of my *home*. A man rushes toward me and I step back in fear, though he looks like he wants to help me, for some reason.

"This way, please, Miss Finnegan," he says, grabbing my shoulder and taking me through the crowd of people as he pushes them away.

"I'm so sorry," I say when I bump into someone.

The man opens a black SUV for me, and because I'm so disoriented, I rush to get in. Instantly, pain ripples through my ass, making it uncomfortable to sit. Even now, in the midst of chaos, the pain is reminding me of Rowan. This is exactly what he wanted, I realize.

The man closes the door behind me, and although the buzz is gone, now I'm feeling the fear creep in. Who is he? He could be anyone, and I just entered his car like I know him. *Fuck.*

"Are you all right?" he asks me when he gets into the driver's seat.

I nod. "Yes, I think so. I'm sorry, who are you?"

"Zain Khan. I work for the commander. Myself along with my team will be escorting you wherever you need to be," he says, driving us away from the paparazzi. "When you're at home, we'll be stationed around your apartment. But don't worry, we'll keep our distance. You won't even know we're there."

"Oh."

When Rowan told me he'd place some of his men around my apartment, I didn't expect it to happen in a matter of a few hours. A small warning would've been nice. Though when I take my phone out of my purse, I see that the message I received is from him. When did he even input his contact into my phone?

"Go with Zain, he'll take you wherever you need to be," the message says.

"What's with all the paparazzi????" I text back. *"It's crazy. It was just a picture!"*

"Your fault. If you weren't so goddamn beautiful..." He trails off, and I roll my eyes despite my smile.

"A warning would've been nice. I thought Zain was about to kidnap me."

"Did you think I was going to let you face that crowd on your own? I've got you, angel. You can relax."

"I wish I could. But I'm finding it rather difficult to

sit down at the moment."

"Fuck, angel. Don't make me turn this plane around."

"You're on a plane?? Where are you going?"

For some reason, he doesn't text back anymore. I try not to get in my head about it. If he's on a plane, he probably had to turn it off. Hopefully.

Zain takes me to the office and I spend most of the day looking through depositions and trying to find anything useful for Miss Pratt to use in our case. At lunch time, I go buy us coffee and sandwiches, and I get the constant urge to look behind me for anyone that might follow.

Zain told me he and the others would be watching me from the shadows. But even so, for some reason I can't shake the feeling that my new bodyguards aren't the only ones interested in following my tracks.

TWELVE

A few days pass, and I try to bury myself in work so I don't dread the minutes Rowan isn't here. He's still gone—to London, as I found out by keeping the news channel on. I'm fidgeting with his key right now, debating whether I should just go to his house. Because he's right. Even if he's not there, being surrounded by his environment would still be better than not feeling him around.

My eyes keep sliding over to my phone, expecting a text or a call. I can't help but feel like a teenage girl in love, butterflies in my belly and all. When it vibrates on my desk, I'm quick to grab it in my hands, though disappointment courses through me when I see it's my mom. We've already talked multiple times after she saw my picture on the news.

A rush of heat starts at the top of my head and spreads down my spine. Yes, *that* picture. Where Rowan's hand was all over my pussy, and no one knew. No one but him and me.

"He's in London right now!" my mom texts.

"Stop stalking him," I text back.

"Why aren't you with him? He should've taken you with him."

I roll my eyes, my fingers dashing through the touchscreen keyboard.

"Just because we're together, it doesn't mean I'm going to abandon my life. Got work to do."

"Your dad used to leave me behind all the time. I just hope he isn't like that..."

I clench my jaw, already annoyed at her remark. This happens every single time I mention any man in my life—not that there have been many. She's projecting her insecurities on me and sometimes... I end up projecting them. I don't want that to happen with Rowan, so I cut her off before she gets more ideas to put in my head.

"He isn't. Gotta go. Love you xx"

I put my phone back, though two more messages come through. And I get it—I know she feels lonely after her husband left and her other kid died. But with everything that happened, leaving that town behind was the best thing I could've done for myself. And my mom, as much as I love her, keeps finding ways to drag me right back into the past.

I've asked her to move to Washington with me, but she's still very much attached to that place. Like she's still waiting for my father to come back, even after all these years. I told myself I'm never going to be like that. I'll never wait on a man who doesn't want me, and I'll never beg for what he does not want to offer me freely.

Maybe that's why I haven't texted Rowan yet, even though every fiber of my being is telling me to do so. Why isn't he calling? Why did I have to hear about him being in London from the news?

I get up from my desk and decide to start cleaning: vacuuming, dusting, and mopping every square inch. Cleaning always keeps me centered in the present moment, which is exactly what I need right now. When I'm done, I return to my desk, determined to get a head start on work for next week. That's when my doorbell rings, and I jolt upright like a spring.

I scurry down the hallway on my tiptoes, my pulse quickening.

"Hello?" I say through the closed door. "Who is it?"

"Just me, Zain."

My heart drops a little, but the feeling is completely lost when I open the door and I'm met with the biggest, most beautiful bouquet of white and pink peonies. It's so lush, I can't even see Zain's head behind it.

"Oh my God," I say, inhaling their fresh, sweet aroma that already wafts all over me. "Thank you!" Instinctively, I bring my hand to my chest, huffing a breathy smile as the flowers are slowly pushed toward me.

"I'm merely the messenger, Miss Finnegan," he smiles.

The flowers are heavy in my arms, their curly, soft petals smearing my skin with early summer mist. My phone rings on the table again, and I turn my head toward the sound. I glance over at Zain.

"I..."

"I'll be around," Zain says, nodding softly as he retreats into the shadows, where he and his team are watching over me. They've been here ever since Rowan left, and I kind of feel bad because there's nothing for them to do. Which is also a good thing, I suppose, since that means no one's trying to get to me.

I close the door and pick up the call, my heart desperate to get out of my chest as I see Rowan's name across the screen. I bring it up to my ear, but his husky voice envelops me before I get to say hello.

"Look outside. Through your main window."

Pushing my lower lip between my teeth, I rush toward it with the flowers still in my arms, expecting to see him out front. But I pull my transparent curtains to the side, and I'm met with the sight of another bouquet of peonies that one of Zain's men is holding in front of a black car.

"Rowan..." I smile.

"Get in the car, angel," he commands.

"Are you back from London?"

"No."

"Then why—"

"You have exactly ten minutes to go downstairs and get into the car. If you're not there when I call again, I'm going to punish you when I get back—and I promise it is *not* the kind you'll look forward to."

I suck in a breath, nervousness creeping in. With Rowan, I never know what to expect. Sex is never gentle with him, and although I love it, it makes me actually concerned what his punishments would entail.

"Is that understood?"

"Y-Yes. Yes, sir."

The call ends without another word, and I look around me for what to do next. The flowers. I have to put the flowers in a vase or something.

I run toward the kitchen, palms sweating and heat curling up on my skin. I get a vase out and put them in with a load of water. Then I change into a white skirt and flowery top, and lock up before hurrying downstairs.

The elevator isn't working this week—the management has yet to fix it. So I huff and puff all the way to the first floor when it hits me. I forgot to pack the sexy lingerie I bought the other day to surprise him. I look at the time on my phone and see that I've still got four minutes left of the time Rowan allowed me. Cursing internally, I decide to make a run for it, back to the fifth floor.

I unlock my door and burst into the hallway, not bothering to take off my shoes. There. On the bedroom floor, in the pink-striped Victoria's Secret shopping bag. I bend down to snatch it and when I head back out into the living room... I freeze.

There's a half-peeled blood orange on my side table.

Its juice has splattered over the glass, staining it, as if whoever peeled it wasn't gentle when holding it between their fingers. The thought of someone else being here is terrifying, but I don't remember eating an orange today. Or buying one, even.

The hairs on the back of my neck stand up. I look toward the main door, my heart slamming against my ribcage. Fear, true unfiltered fear bolts through my body like lightning, my head feeling foggy from the rush of hormones.

"I have a gun," I lie, forcing my voice to come out stronger than how I feel. "And I'm not afraid to use it."

Silence. Only the ticking clock in my hallway and my blood whooshing in my ears fill the space.

"Zain!" I shout, my voice now shaky and rough. "Zain!"

I swallow a sob and decide to make a run for the door. Just then, Zain's body bumps into mine, and he shoves me behind him as I tremble like a leaf. Fuck, I really should go to those self-defense classes I've been meaning to try.

"Stay here," he says, pulling out his gun and disappearing behind the walls of my home. Behind me, two more of his men are approaching, all carrying guns and pointing them over my shoulder. I don't move a muscle as they walk by me.

After a few moments, Zain gets back with his gun tucked in.

"What happened?" he asks. "There's no one inside."

That's impossible. Unless... unless my memory is failing me, and I did eat that orange. But...

"I'm... I'm sorry. Are you sure... have you checked everywhere?"

"Yes. Everywhere someone might be able to hide. We're trained for this exact type of situation. So trust me, Miss Finnegan, there is no one in your home other than my team right now."

What the hell?

"Thank you. I'm so sorry, I thought—"

"What happened?" he presses on, pinning me with his gaze. His men come around him, their guns also tucked back into place.

"I think I'm just tired and... on edge, with everything going on. I'm not used to being followed by the paparazzi or people trying to take selfies with me. I'm so sorry."

"You do not have to apologize. This is what we're here to do. I should call the commander."

"*No*! Please, don't! This is so embarrassing... I don't want him to worry for nothing. Please?"

Zain studies me for a few moments as I put on the biggest puppy eyes I can. Finally, he sighs, and my entire body relaxes with it.

"Very well, then, Miss Finnegan. But you have to promise you'll call out for us if anything else looks suspicious, even if it turns out being nothing. Do we have a deal?"

"Dove," I say, extending my hand forward. "Please, call me Dove. And sure, that should be okay. Though I promise to get some rest so my mind doesn't play tricks on me next time."

Zain nods softly and exits my apartment together with his men on his trail. I let loose a temporary sigh of relief, the whole situation still having me on edge. I didn't eat that orange. And unless Zain's men were inside my apartment when I wasn't there... I have no fucking clue who did. Fuck, maybe I really am tired. Maybe this whole thing is taking a toll on me. I'll deal with this when I get back.

The phone rings again just when Zain's teammate

opens the door to the SUV for me, in front of my apartment.

"Hey. I'm in the car right now." I try to keep my tone positive, despite the unease still roiling in my gut. "What are we doing?"

Unfortunately though, Rowan sees right through me, like he always does.

"What happened?" he asks, his tone like gravel softened by thunderous rain. The sound of his voice settles low in my bones, gnawing at me with concern.

I sigh, closing the car's door behind me. "I'm just a bit tired. Who thought taking so many selfies with strangers over the past few days would wear me out like this?" I chuckle.

A deadly pause, and then, "You're lying to me. Why?"

I stutter, shame washing over me at the disappointment in his words. I *am* lying to him.

"I'm..." I sigh, looking out the tinted window. "I really didn't want to worry you for nothing. I thought I saw something or... someone in my apartment. But Zain—"

"Zain didn't call back to report this."

"I kind of asked him not to. You have a lot on your mind right now, and I didn't want to—"

"Oh, angel..." He scoffs a laugh that drags a whimper through the length of my throat. "We really do need to work on your training, don't we?"

"I..."

"When I ask you something, I expect you to be honest with me. I don't care if you think you have the right reasons to lie. You do *not* worry about me. Not now, not ever. But me? I will turn this world upside down to protect what's mine. And lest you forget it, angel, you do belong to me now. Do you not?"

"Rowan... I'm really..."

"Answer me."

"Yes, I belong to you now."

"Splendid. I will take care of this small interference later. *Now*... there's a black box on the seat next to you. Pick it up," he says, directing my attention to the object. He's so blunt today—more so than usual. I wonder if everything is all right with him.

"What is this?"

"A suction device. For your pussy."

"Oh."

I can sense the dark smile on his face as he continues, "Turn it on, and put it under your skirt until Perez drives you to your destination."

How does he know I'm wearing a skirt? My cheeks flush with heat as I take the object out of the box, inspecting it. It's shaped like a pink rose, and I can't help but press my thighs together imagining the way it would feel sucking on my sensitive clit.

"But Perez... I can't possibly do that with him in the car."

"You can, and you will. Stay still and don't let him see it. This is for me and no one else. I'm watching you right now, and I want to see you squirm on that seat until he drops you off."

"Rowan..." I plead, though if I'm being honest, I kind of want to go through with it. He's watching me right now? Well then, I'm going to give him a good fucking show.

"Lift up your skirt, Dove. Or I'll make you."

I burn at the dominance in his voice while simultaneously fidgeting with the ends of my skirt, pulling it up a few inches. My naked legs pebble with goose bumps and my pussy pulses in anticipation of submitting to him.

"Show me your pussy. Pull your panties to the side."

My fingers stroke my pussy through my thong, darting out to the side where I can pull the fabric away to reveal the soft bundle of nerves between my legs. I'm already so wet.

"Fuck," Rowan grunts. His voice gets louder, as if he's approaching the phone, trying to join me here on this seat.

"Yes," I moan in response, mimicking his reaction as I press my fingers to my pussy, arching my back like a cat.

"Turn it on. Press the toy to your slit. Hard. As if I'm there, pushing my tongue into you."

I do as he says, my head dipping back from the heat that's curling at the base of my spine, driving pleasure all throughout my core. My walls clench around nothing, the toy sucking me in like it's indeed Rowan's mouth licking all over my starved pussy. I lean back, huffing out air with every deep stroke, every tendril of pleasure that makes my legs shake as my orgasm builds up inside me.

"Press your thighs together around the toy. Remove your hand and pull your skirt back over your pussy. I'm sending Perez in the car right now."

"No, please, wait—ahhh."

"Now, Dove. Or he'll see you come all over your hands, and then I'll have no choice but to pluck out his eyeballs. Do you understand?"

"You wouldn't..." I gasp, pressing the toy harder to my slit, my hips buckling to the point where I'm now riding it.

"I would do far worse if another man ever saw you like that without my permission. Perez means nothing to me. You mean everything."

The car stops in front of Rowan's house, and Perez is the first to get out—thank God. I'm all flushed, wet, and needy for Rowan as the toy keeps sucking between my legs like a starved, sentient being.

Hesitantly, I take it out of my pussy and put it back in the small box, willing my shaky legs to move and keep me upright as I step outside on the pavement.

Rowan hasn't called again, so I'm not sure why he wanted me here, at his house, in the spur of the moment. I make my way into the living room, the door already unlocked for me. But no sooner do I make it inside when... I feel it.

The scent. And the warm breeze that carries it from the garden through the open sliding doors, wrapping around my body like a second skin.

I inch toward it, shaking my head in disbelief for what I know to be true even without seeing it yet.

Hundreds—no, *thousands*—of peonies must be waiting on the other side of this curtain that's flapping above the glass doors. That's the only possible way you get a naturally sweet scent that is this strong to fill the air.

"Oh my God," I exhale when I step through the doors into Rowan's garden.

The field is literally filled with peonies as far as my eyes can see, stretching around the tall willow trees, the pond, and the lush bushes. It looks like a huge cloud of pink and white silk, and I rush toward them, my skirt swirling around me when I spin in place, taking it all in.

My phone rings again.

"Whatever you need to feel at home in this house, I'll bring it to you. All you have to do is ask," Rowan says.

"Still want me to move in with you, huh?"

His voice lowers. "I want everything with you." I'm taken aback by the confession.

"How... how can you know for sure, when you've just met me?"

"One day, I'll show you everything. Everything I am, and everything you mean to me. Until then, I want to come home to my entire house smelling like my perfect angel and nothing else."

"Would that make you happy?"

"Feral is more like it."

I pause for a few moments, taking in the view as I

clutch the phone with both hands.

"Rowan?"

"Yes, angel?"

"I know you said not to worry about you. But I do worry. It's hard not to, knowing the kind of job you have. You seem a bit... different today. And I just wanted to make sure you're okay."

He sighs, a hint of a smile audible through this breathing. "I never realized letting someone in would mean that they too would start reading me well. I'll tell you, since you'll hear it on the news anyway. There's been an attack on the Ridge. One that doesn't make any sense. In fact, it's almost as if they're trying to distract us from something else. It's why I can't come home tonight, like I wanted to. Even so, is there a chance you'll agree to spend the night in our bed?"

I take in what he's telling me but I don't press him on it. Even my brother wasn't allowed to tell us much about the war, and he wasn't as high up in the ranks as Rowan is.

"If I say yes, does that mean I'll wake up in your arms tomorrow?"

"I hate to spoil part of the surprise, but yes, there's something important I need to do tomorrow. And I'm taking you with me."

"What is it?" I walk across the porch, watching a wild duck land in the nearby pond, a few soft waves cresting in the wake of its flapping wings.

"We're meeting the President and the First Lady in the Oval Office for lunch."

THIRTEEN

The first thing I sense is heat. Rowan is pressed against me from behind, his hot flesh covering my ass and thighs. His hands roam over my body and I feel myself quivering under his touch. My dream is so vivid—similar to the ones I used to have after meeting him for the first time.

My face is pressed into the bed, my moans being smothered by the mattress as he slides his hard cock up and down in the crack of my ass. The sensation of his massive errection feels so real that I'm starting to think this is not actually a dream at all.

Slowly I start to become more aware of sounds filtering into my awareness. The sleek echo of my arousal fills the silence, tangled with the heavy, sexy-as-fuck breathing of the man I'm obsessed with.

I wake up to strong arms pinning me down, fingers digging into my hips. My body hikes up and down, rumpling the sheets under my naked skin while Rowan's cock slides in and out of my pussy from behind.

"Row-ah—" His name barely rolls off my tongue as all my senses come back to life. How long has he been fucking me? What time is it?

"Shhh, angel. I'm not done using your pretty holes."

I want to kiss him, feel him in my mouth. But when I try to turn on my back, I realize I'm stuck. My wrists are crossed and tied together with thick rope above my lower back. That same rope trails down across my breasts, grazing my already hard nipples, then goes down to my waist, securing my ankles to my thighs.

My legs are practically parted to the max, exposing me—all of me—to Rowan, who uses my pussy the way he wants. I'm panting, my body shaking and clit throbbing with need as all the knots rub against my skin.

I move my head to the right as best I can, lifting my eyes to catch Rowan's raven-colored hair that's swaying every time he thrusts inside me. I flinch with a soft cry when I feel his thumb pressing into my ass, entering me through there as well.

"Please..." I whimper, ashamed that I'm rocking my hips into his cock at the same time he's thrusting into me. My hair is pulled back in one rapid stroke and my head lifts off the mattress. I roll my eyes to the back of my skull, catching his gaze boring into mine.

"No need to feel shy now. Not after my tongue was all up in your sweet cunt."

My pussy clamps down on his hard cock, cheeks burning as his words scurry down my nerve endings, making me whimper and lick my lips. The tight grip he has on my hair makes my scalp hurt, causing fresh tears to swarm at the corners of my eyes. Not from the pain, but from the pleasure coursing through me that's making me realize new things about my body and my needs.

"Am I hurting you?"

I moan first, then I say, "Yeah."

"Good. Then maybe you'll think twice about lying to me next time."

I want to tell him no just to see what else he'll do to me. But I don't get to when he bends down to lick the side of my neck, his tongue darting out slowly, leaving goosebumps in its wake.

"I have no problem blocking out the entire morning to claim every part of your body with my tongue and teeth. It's up to you."

"Up to me?" I pant, my voice scattered as I keep being raised up and down while he fucks my pussy from behind. I'm so drenched right now. I'm so close. Everything hurts, and yet I'm so close to coming all over his cock.

"Mm-hmm. I want you to get it into your head that you do not lie to me. That you do not *worry* about upsetting me with your honesty. You are not allowed. Because if you do..."

His cock throbs inside me, spilling his cum between my walls and filling me up. He wants to see me when he's claiming me like this. He wants me unable to look anywhere else but into his eyes.

My head falls back on the soft pillow when he lets go, my hair now in my mouth and eyes and sticking to the sides of my face from the light sheen of sweat trickling across my skin. A sharp slap lands on my ass, and Rowan slides two fingers inside my pussy, pushing back the cum that's now leaking out.

Rowan's free arm pushes my neck deeper into the pillow, his veins poking through his tanned skin as he wraps his fingers around my throat.

"...then I'll simply remind you again." *Thrust.* "And again." *Thrust.* "And again. In ways I don't think you'll be eager to find out."

"If I want to lie," I breathe out, feeling my orgasm creeping up on me. "I'll lie." I smirk, my lips stretching against the sheets.

"That so?" he says, followed by a dark chuckle so low it rumbles through my body, making my insides tremble with need. "Then let's fix that fucking attitude of yours right now. Because you should know better, Dove... you should know so much better than to provoke me like this."

Another thrust is all it takes until I clamp down on his fingers, riding my release. My legs twitch and jolt uncontrollably as if an earthquake shakes the entire universe with me in it. My walls throb around his fingers, desperate to trap him inside. The cum he pushed inside me mixes with mine, and it's all a sloppy mess inside my drenched pussy while he continues to finger-fuck me through it like he doesn't give a damn I just came with everything I had.

"Oh my God," I cry out, my pussy going completely numb.

I yelp when he turns me on my back, my hands and

thighs supporting my weight beneath me as I'm spread out like a starfish for him. He moves to untie one of the knots above my stomach so I get the impression this is over for now. But the subtle lift of the corner of his mouth gives it away—he's nowhere near done.

Rowan pulls the rope down between my legs, tying another knot to secure it between my pussy lips and ass cheeks. I call out his name as it's now grazing against my most sensitive spot, drawing painful tendrils of pleasure out of it. My toes curl at the new sensation, and I start grinding my pussy on the tight rope.

My lips part with a moan, and Rowan's fingers surprise me when they push inside my mouth, all the way to the back. I gag on them, but he keeps them there, unmoving, while I try to calm down.

"Breathe through your nose. Relax your jaw."

I follow his eyes with mine, chest rising and lowering as I try my best to follow the instructions. Just like never having my ass fucked before, I've never given someone a blowjob. I worry I won't be able to take him, knowing how big he is. But he continues to prove me wrong every time. If it doesn't fit, he'll make it fit.

Something sweet and salty spreads out on my tongue when I finally relax, and I realize it's our cum from when his fingers were in my pussy. Involuntarily, I close my lips around his fingers and suck, my lips soft against the rough intrusion.

"Fucking hell," Rowan curses as he starts fucking my mouth. "You like having your mouth fucked, angel? Is this making you wet?"

I wouldn't know what to answer him even if I could.

I am enjoying it, aren't it? I love being filled by him, and I don't care which hole he chooses. Everywhere he touches, bites, or smacks, I am becoming obsessed with it.

I'm spun around and my head hangs off the edge of the bed, Rowan's hard cock inching closer to my mouth. "Then open wide. I'm going to give you a chance to earn your forgiveness."

His fingers retract and I try to take in huge heaps of air, but Rowan pushes himself between my lips faster than I can blink. He's big and hard, and when he reaches the back of my throat, I start gagging again. The sound is loud and dirty, and it makes him smile down on me. Then he stops, letting me adjust to him, his head dipped back and eyes closing slowly as he chases his own high.

"You think you're cute," he laughs.

Thrust.

"Lying to me... defying me like you don't know what I'm made of."

Thrust.

"Look at you now, angel. Crying with a mouthful of cock—*my* cock. Drooling all over it like a filthy, filthy girl. Not so cute anymore, are we?"

Holding my chin in place with one hand and the top of my head with the other, he fucks my mouth rough and hard, grunting and moaning while I do exactly what he describes—crying, drooling, and leaking with arousal from that rope digging into my pussy.

As if on cue, Rowan pulls on it and I cry out, the pain and the pleasure intensifying. My wrists are numb at this point, and so are my ankles. There's probably no blood going through them right now as I lie here with my head upside down, gagging on his cock.

"Will you lie to me again?"

I choke out a "no" but I'm not sure he understands me.

"I can't hear you, Dove. My cock is still buried in your warm mouth."

Fresh tears fall on my cheeks, mixing with the drool running down my chin. I look up at him, pleading eyes and all, while I repeat the word again, and again, and again like a chant.

I won't lie. I'll never lie again.

His dark laugh fills the room, and then I feel his warm seed spill down my throat. I look up at him while I swallow, his expression feral and ready to go another round.

"I won't," I say, just to make sure he got it, with my voice rough and dry. "I won't lie. I'm so sorry," I sob.

"I know you are, angel," he coos, untying the rope that sits between my pussy lips and caressing my red and swollen clit with his long finger, dulling out the pain. I shiver under his touch, licking traces of him off my lips and swallowing those too. "Now let's make this pussy come one last time. Yes?"

"It... hurts. My wrists hurt."

"I know they do. You'll be free as soon as you come again. Just one more, angel. Can you give me one more?" He asks it, yet he already knows the answer. My pussy arches upward, chasing his finger, wanting it to add more pressure to my clit.

"That's it." He slides his finger across my clit, drawing soft circles around it while he pinches my nipple with the other hand. "Such a good girl. Let go, angel."

His fingers travel down to the entrance of my pussy, smearing my wetness back around my clit. I'm throbbing everywhere, my legs shaking and chest heaving with shallow breaths.

"Come for me."

I cry out, eyes snapping shut while my pussy clamps down on his finger one last time, pulsing with a shorter—but still very much intense—release. I come down gradually, feeling my entire body ache and loosen at the same time. I feel sweaty and dirty everywhere. But when I open my eyes, Rowan still looks at me like I'm the most beautiful woman this world has ever seen.

After he cradled me in his arms and let me cry into the crook of his neck while he bathed me, Rowan helped me get dressed in this beautiful misty rose-pink dress that he bought me as a surprise. It's a silky slip-dress designed with a drapey neckline, a stem-showing side vent, and an open back. It molds perfectly to my body, accentuating just the right places.

"Ready?" he asks, caressing my hand with his thumb.

We're about to meet the President and the First Lady of the United States. And once we get out of the car, we're going to have to rush past all the photographers and journalists who somehow found out we were having this meeting today.

"I'm actually really nervous. I can't believe we're doing this."

"Don't be. They're just like you and me. In fact, we probably have more in common than you think."

"Like what?"

He smirks. "You'll see."

"Wait!" I touch his arm before he gets a chance to open the car's door. "There's something I wanted to ask you. About Zain..."

Rowan's brows arch up as he pins me with his gaze. "What about him?"

"Just that it wasn't his fault. So please don't be hard on him. I made him promise not to tell you about the incident at my house, which turned out to be nothing, thank God."

"Don't worry about it. I already fired him."

"You... you what?"

Guilt settles heavily on my chest, making me frown.

"He was given an order. And he willingly went against it. So I fired him. Now—"

"No! I told you it was my fault, not his! This is completely unnecessary. Please, Rowan..."

I shake my head, frustration roiling in my gut and wanting to come out, to lash out at him. What if Zain had a family to care for? What if he worked all his life for that job? For Rowan to just take it away from him like that...

"It is not your fault that a grown man who knew the consequences of his insubordination willingly chose to go against direct orders. The safety of the woman I love is on the line, and I am *not* about to start cutting corners when I know so many things could go wrong while I'm away. So yes, even if it turned out to be nothing, he should've fucking told me about what happened. I always need to be in the know."

The woman he... *loves*?

Goddamn him and that gifted mouth. Butterflies are already coming to life in my stomach, and it's really fucking hard to be upset with him. But I don't think it's right. Firing Zain was unnecessary. Nothing happened at my apartment. No one was there. Right?

"I'm going to open the door now. And we're going to step outside. I'll take your hand and guide you through the crowd. Okay, angel?"

"Fine," I say, keeping my tone neutral, though I don't fail to notice the subtle smirk he flashes before stepping out of the car. His hand dips back inside, open and inviting, wanting me to come out with him.

What a prick he is being right now. He's enjoying this. He wants me to talk back. Almost as if he's looking forward to punishing me again. Well, if he wants to play that kind of game, I'm all here for it. Consequences be damned.

FOURTEEN

Escaping the paparazzi wasn't any easier this time. But with Rowan by my side, I felt a lot more empowered—and safe. Hell, I even smiled when someone called my name and I turned my face so they could take my picture. If this is my life now, might as well try to roll with it.

Rowan's wide palm holds me close to his body as he leads us inside the White House, a trail of men in black suits following a few steps behind. I crook my neck upward to take in the white sandstone pillars, the perfect curves of the balconies, and the detailed garland decorations. It's a massive structure, and I've only ever seen it on TV or from very far away.

To think I'm actually going inside, to visit the President *and* the First Lady while accompanied by the Commander of the Army is insane. What if I make a fool of myself? Or worse... what if I somehow embarrass him in front of them?

I almost trip on my heels before Rowan steadies me

with a hand behind my lower back, flashing me a lazy smile. I look back at him for a brief second. He's calm. Too calm for this.

"Rowan..." I start, the words stuck somewhere in my throat, unwilling to come out. But the look on his face tells me he already knows what's on my mind. I love how well he knows me already.

He stops walking to stand in front of me, and everyone else follows suit.

I look around, feeling like I'm under a microscope as staff members buzz across the hallway, each doing their job.

"Lips," he says, cupping my face and bringing it in toward his. I release a shallow breath, his forehead touching mine as I close my eyes, feeling safe in the small space he created between our bodies. "Give me your lips, pretty girl."

I inch closer, our lips brushing each other before I press mine to his and I whimper into his mouth, inhaling his cologne and his warmth.

"Don't even think about it. I brought you here so I can show off with you. There's no possible way you can embarrass me. So show me your pretty smile, give me your hand, and let me introduce you to my friends. Yes?"

I nod, pursing my lips, with my eyebrows knitted in worry.

"Good girl," he says, and we start walking again.

"Fucking hell." Draven Grant—the Secretary of State—approaches with a file tucked under his armpit, hands in his pockets as he grins with perfectly white teeth. "Every time I see you, I ask myself, how is this bastard still alive?"

He laughs, and Rowan snorts playfully, shaking hands with him without letting go of mine.

"If you still have to ask yourself that, it means I haven't given Maddox enough headaches this year. Guess I'll fix that today," Rowan says.

"Oh, believe me, the President has been stressed as fuck. Especially since he heard about the order you have over the prisoners from the Ridge. You're a crazy son of a bitch."

Rowan smirks. "It's good to see you too. Dove, this is my good friend, Draven. He's—"

"The Secretary of State," I add, flashing him a smile. "Of course, I knew that. It's a pleasure to meet you, sir."

A pause, and then Rowan's hand tenses on mine, as if I did something wrong. Fuck, did I? When I catch his gaze, his eyes are feral and his nostrils flared as he plasters a dark, knowing smile on his face.

"A pleasure indeed," Draven chimes in, but doesn't go past my face with his eyes. I take it as a sign of respect toward Rowan.

"Are they in there?" Rowan jerks his head to the doors leading into the Oval Office. I gulp, trying my hardest to smile and look perfect for him, even though my anxiety is through the roof right now.

"Mm-hmm," Draven sighs. "I had to make sure *twice* they weren't fucking last minute or... giving each other black eyes."

"Now that would be a sight."

Confusion coils around me at Draven's words.

Maddox and Camelia Thorne love each other. They've been America's favorite couple ever since they got married last year, after Maddox's ex-wife passed away. Why would Draven joke about them giving each other black eyes?

"This way, angel." Rowan gets my attention, gently pulling me after him as someone opens doors to the Oval Office for us.

The first thing I see is the carpet, because looking straight ahead and meeting their faces is not as easy as I thought it'd be. So I look down at the famous Presidential carpet and at my heels stepping on it for the first time. Then I hear their voices—his, Rowan's, and hers—before Rowan's hand caresses the small of my back, and I regain my composure.

Icy blue eyes, collected and observing, stare back at me when I look up. I force a big smile, taken aback by how much more imposing Maddox Thorne is in real life. He's huge—just as tall as Rowan, if I'm judging it right—maybe somewhere around six-foot-five. And with a lush mouth and a sharp jawline like that, it's not hard to see how he won the hearts of millions of Americans at such a young age. He's what... 36 now?

I relax a little when he smiles back, his features instantly warming up. Even the walls seemed to have breathed a sigh of relief for me.

"Thank God. Someone finally managed to tame Rowan," the President smirks, his voice like the ebb and flow of ocean waves, powerful yet calming, with a rhythmic cadence that pulls you in and holds you captive.

To my surprise, I chuckle, and do the unimaginable—contradict him.

"I hate to disappoint, but I don't see that happening anytime soon, Mr. President."

A generous laugh approaching from behind him gets my attention. It sounds like the crackle of a cozy fireplace, warm and inviting, with a playful flicker that promises things you probably shouldn't crave. Camelia Thorne—or Cam, as he calls her publicly, comes to the President's side, arms crossed as she stares me down.

The tabloids almost don't do her justice for how insanely gorgeous she is. It's not even her wavy beach-blonde hair or the muted, ashy green color of her eyes that makes her so effortlessly chic and timeless. It's the way she carries herself, with the calm and elegance of a feline who knows she has the claws and the fangs to kill if anything threatens her way of life.

It's also the subtle ways she glances over at her husband with her thick web of long lashes—as if she loathes him, or loathes that she *wants* him so goddamn much.

She doesn't brush her body against his when she stands next to him. If anything, she looks like she's doing everything in her power *not* to touch him. But then the President looks back at her... and the tension between them bounces between the four of us. It keeps building and building, until my face heats up and I feel like I should give them the privacy they so desperately seem to need.

"Damn right," Cam says, finally breaking her husband's stare. "Rowan is a tough one to crack. Most of us have completely given up trying to fix him."

"Nonsense." Rowan waves a hand in the air, leading us both toward the couch. "You love me. There's already a serious bastard among us." He eyes the President. "Can't have two people sitting in the same chair, now, can we?"

"Wouldn't dream of it." Maddox rolls his eyes, and the two of them take their own seats across from us. "This job is stressful enough as it is. Convincing *you* not to kill people is, to be exact."

"It had to be done, and you know it."

"Word could still get out."

"That's why you have a whole PR department at your fingertips."

"It's not"—the President sighs—"that easy."

"When was anything easy about what we do?"

The President and the Commander of his Army stare each other down, while Cam and I look between them. I hold my breath under the tension, while she seems to hold back from snorting. Then she glances over at me and mouths the word "typical." I purse my lips, relaxing a little.

"So..." I say, getting their attention, "how was your trip to Vermont? I saw it on the news."

Cam laughs, leaning back on the couch with her legs crossed. "I like you. You seem quiet and reserved, but you've got a fire in you of sorts. We're going to be friends."

"We are?" I ask, surprised she likes me so much.

"She's already decided it, so yes, I'm afraid you two *are* going to be friends," Rowan says, narrowing his eyes at her. She responds by plastering a Cheshire smile on her lips.

We talk and eat lunch for a full hour. They both ask about my job, my life, and my life with Rowan. I try to ask questions of my own—though it's hard to come up with any when most of their lives are so public all the time. Either way, I'm honestly having a pretty good time, considering all the nerves I had earlier.

For some reason, I noticed that Cam keeps touching her necklace whenever the President touches her in any way, shape, or form. I wish we could talk about it—she seems like a genuinely great person, and I hope she meant it when she said she wanted to be friends.

"Cam, why don't you take Dove and show her around? Maybe take her to the rose garden, or the Vermeil room?" The President—I mean, *Maddox*, as he asked to be called—tells her, his hand sliding up and down her bare leg. Goosebumps pebble her skin wherever he touches, and both her cheeks are blood-red. I also could've sworn her legs parted slightly for him, but I could be wrong.

"Great idea." She clears her throat, jolting upright from the couch. "Come on, Dove. It's about to get really depressing in here."

I look back at Rowan, feeling a bit anxious about leaving his side in the White House. But he nods softly, silently telling me it's going to be all right.

"What do you mean?" I ask her, but Rowan answers instead.

"Just war stuff, angel. Go on. Have fun. I'll come and get you when I'm done."

I get up and follow Cam outside, feeling both Rowan's and Maddox's eyes on us.

"Cam?" Maddox asks, and she halts, lifting her brows at him.

"Yes, Mr. President?"

"Behave," he smiles calmly. "Or be prepared for consequences. Up to you."

Her nostrils flare in response, but she forces a smile before we both exit the room.

I'm sprawled on a chair in an empty salon three blocks away from the White House, where the First Lady and I are getting our nails done. After whatever subtext Maddox gave her earlier, she wanted to do the exact opposite of what he asked—to *not* behave. Which for her meant getting out of the White House and enjoying the day with her new friend. Me.

Security already cleared the place for her and surrounded the building, so we're as safe as we'd be anywhere else, she said. I personally don't feel threatened—after all, I still go about my day-to-day life outside of the White House. It's her I'm worried about. But if she says it's fine, then...

"Fired your bodyguard? That's pretty tame," Cam tells me after I confessed the reason I was mad at Rowan earlier. "You should see the things Maddox does. He's *infuriating.*"

"Is he? You can't really tell. He looks… friendly."

She sighs, inspecting the polished nails on her free hand. "Yeah, well, that's his superpower. Everyone just *loooves* Maddox. I mean, look at this country. Zelda," she addresses the woman doing her nails, "don't you love your president?"

"Of course, ma'am."

"Ah, but maybe you're just saying that because *I'm* here," Cam concludes, looking away.

"No, ma'am. He's done good things for our country."

"See?" Cam shakes her head at me, exasperated. "What did I tell you?"

I stifle a laugh, while silently thanking my manicurist for finishing off my second coat of polish.

"You have to give me something," I tell Cam. "What does Maddox do that Rowan doesn't?"

Cam clears her throat and points at the necklace she's wearing when the manicurists aren't looking. It's tight on her neck, almost too tight, and looks like a choker of sorts. An odd choice for the First Lady, one would say. Then again, Camelia Thorne is loved by this country for her eccentric personality.

"A collar," she mouths silently.

I gape, taken aback by the confession. A… collar?

The two women get up from their stations and clear the room for us, letting us wait for the polish to dry.

"Maddox and I have a… complicated relationship. It's not what you see on the news," she tells me, still in a quiet voice.

"Oh. I'm sorry to hear. Again, you…"

"You can't really tell?" she finishes the sentence for me. "Pretending is part of the job. It's what we do."

"You don't love him?"

An intrusive question, no doubt. I won't be surprised if she chooses not to answer.

"I… it's complicated. Our marriage was very practical to begin with. It pissed my father off. And that's what we both wanted. Look, I don't know how much Rowan told you about our world, but there's probably something you should know."

"He told me bits and pieces. He told me what really happened to my brother, Cole."

"I'm sorry about that, by the way."

"It's okay," I smile. "It's not easy, but I think it's time I finally moved on."

Cam bites her lower lip, looking down into her lap as if she's deciding whether to keep going or not. But then she looks back up, and the words coming out of her mouth are not what I expected to hear today.

Or any other day, for that matter.

"My father was the one who gave the order to kill your brother. He's the leader of the Echelons of the Free World."

FIFTEEN

The old ache settles in my chest, the way it always does whenever Cole's death is brought up. Which seems to be a lot more frequent these days than ever before. What didn't I know about my brother? What's going on in this country that the public has no idea about?

Even without knowing much about this organization they speak of, I realize now that the heart of our society pulses with dark secrets and lies I never dared to imagine—the kind you see in movies and stuff. The facade of normalcy slowly shatters around me, leaving me with a gnawing sense of dread and unshakable unease.

Sucking in a breath, I tilt my head at an angle, my eyes sliding over to Cam's as I say, "Doesn't that mean... you're part of that organization too?" I glance over at the door, my pulse quickening as I connect the dots. The President told her to behave. Now she's telling me this... so Cam probably lured me here, away from everyone's eyes, so she can—

"*Dove*," she says, placing a hand over mine. I jolt, releasing the air trapped in my lungs as fear takes over. "I'm married to the President. I'm wearing his shock collar, for God's sake. Do you really think Rowan would've let you come with me if I were a threat?"

No, no he wouldn't. Unless... unless he has no idea.

But it's hard to believe he isn't in the know about stuff like this.

"You just told me you're involved in the murder of my brother. How am I supposed to... What am I supposed to do with this information?"

"I said my *father* was. And I only told you so that it doesn't take you by surprise after we're already deep into this friendship," she sighs. "I was born into the EFW. For a long time, I had no choice but to serve at the shrine of my father's power. The things they do, Dove... you wouldn't wish them on your worst enemies. They run the banks, the courthouses, the education system, the pharmaceutical industry... everything. And people like you and me? We're just like puppets on a string to them. Numbers. Cattle, if you will."

"Even you?" I ask, realizing that I'm practically squeezing her hand between mine. She squeezes mine back, and the gesture embraces me in a sheer layer of temporary placidness.

She nods. "I try to do what I can from this position, but my impact is limited. I can do all the humanitarian work in the world, but if the EFW wants people to die, they'll die. They *do* die, in fact. Every single day. From wars. From cancers with no cure in sight. From accidents that aren't truly accidents, just to make sure someone more important steers clear of crimes committed in their past."

Tears pool around Cam's stormy irises, as if the doors of her heart burst open under the pressure of everything she's been through, unable to contain it anymore. She blinks them away, waving her hand in the air as the smell of acetone from her freshly-painted nails wafts between us.

"It's not fair. And it hurts so much—knowing I get to live this life while so many others suffer under my father's thumb. If it wasn't for Maddox I would've probably been dead by now. I should be, in fact. And I am truly sorry, Dove, for everything we've put you through. For taking away someone you loved so much—" I lean in, placing my other hand over hers as if we're old friends from high school reconnecting after long years.

"I think... I think whatever horrors you went through, Cam, trumps any heartache one can have. It's not your fault. And thank you for trusting me enough to share this with me. People talk about these things, you know. Conspiracy theorists and all. But to think that this is the reality we live in..."

"You should be careful," she says, heaving out a long sigh. "Being with Rowan puts you even higher on their hit list now. They're always looking for ways to weaken our party so they can put someone else at the top—someone they can maneuver the way they want. Why aren't you living with him, by the way? Do I have to fucking spell it out for him? I know he's got a lot on his plate these days, but seriously—"

"No, no, he's actually asked me. Twice. I just... don't want to push him away by being there all the time, you know?"

"That's stupid, and it can get you killed. Listen to me. You need to pack your stuff and go live with him for a while. The man is clearly obsessed with you. You really think he's going to dump you for giving him something he so desperately wants?"

I roll my eyes, puffing a breath as I remember Odette Chevrier and the stupid warning she issued that day when I met her. *Don't give him everything he wants all at once.* It's not that I intentionally wanted to follow her advice. But I guess deep down, I kind of thought she was right.

"This woman... Odette..."

Cam laughs, her head dipping backward as her chest accommodates the generous sound. "*Please*, tell me you aren't doing this because of something Odette Chevrier said to you."

"I mean..."

"Oh my God! Okay, you're in desperate need of some good ol' fashioned Cam advice. That woman is a snake. We don't like her. She does people favors and has everyone wrapped around her finger for when she needs them. But the things she asks for are..." She shakes her head. "Outrageous. One time, she coerced the former Chief of Staff into making her Secretary of State. I don't know the kind of dirt she had on him, but he was forced to *beg* Maddox to appoint her for the role, when she didn't even meet the requirements in the first place."

"I think I read about this online. Speculation only. I didn't know if it was real or not."

She smacks her lips. "It was. This is why the Chief of Staff had to resign. But then we got Reid Cranford hired for the role instead. So in a way, Odette did us all a favor. Anyway… the point is, go take your man, tell him you'll move in with him, and suck him off real good tonight. He'll appreciate it."

"Cam!" I laugh, looking around for any staff that might hear us. "Not so proper for a wildly respected First Lady, are we?"

"Took you long enough to realize that."

I purse my lips, lost in thought as the manicurists come back into the room.

"Anything else we can do for you today, ladies?" one of them asks.

Cam and I look at each other, a secret—and a deeper understanding of one another—binding us closer than we were three hours ago. And I know, just from the way her smile reaches her eyes, that the friendship we developed today will probably last for the rest of our lives.

"Everything all right?" I ask Rowan when he enters the Vermeil room. Cam had to leave to prepare for an interview, so I waited here for him with a tray of chocolate and a glass of wine laid out before me.

I get up from the couch and come to greet him. His jaw is tight, his hair a bit disheveled, and the fact that he keeps silent makes me think it's not just the war planning that has him looking so grave.

His eyes roam over my body hungrily, his hand finding its way through the layers of hair covering my shoulder and pulling me close. I let him do it, approaching with small rapid steps until I crash into his hard chest.

"I missed you," he says in that low voice I love, teasing my lips with his in a soft, tender caress. "I thought having you close by would be easier, but it only made me want you more. Is that crazy?"

"Well, you did say being bat-shit crazy was a prerequisite for earning the highest rank in the military."

His chest rumbles with a hum of approval, making me smile against his lips.

"I was waiting all alone in here, you know..." I slide my hand down his chest, watching his eyes darken in response, a silent question looming behind his irises. "And I was thinking that maybe..."

His chin dips ever so slightly, all his attention on me.

"Maybe moving in with you wouldn't be so bad after all. I've found that you don't snore as loudly as I was picturing it in my head." I grin.

"Oh, really?" He grabs my ass, squeezing hard. "Is that why you haven't so far? Because you thought I snored?"

"That... and the fact that I didn't want to make you get sick of me so quickly. This is still so new. Us."

"You're lucky you said that. Because the punishment I was about to give you for what you did earlier... I'm about to turn it into a sweet reward."

"What? What did I do earlier?" I ponder, though I know the exact moment he's referring to. "And why am I getting a reward?"

Rowan's mouth twitches with a smirk as he grips my chin and tilts my head up, keeping it in place.

"You don't call another man 'sir.' Ever. I don't care if he's an old teacher, a neighbor whose name you don't know, or... *God forbid*, the President."

"That's ridiculous," I laugh, though my breath catches in my throat when the look on his face tells me he's not joking. "What should I call them then?"

"I don't care. You want to use that word so badly, you tell me. I'll bend you over my knee and listen to you say it for as long as you need."

I bite my lower lip, feeling my cheeks burn under his gaze. "And the reward?"

"That's for speaking your mind with me. I hate that you think you could ever make me get sick of you, but I love you for telling me."

"*Love...* me?"

He smiles. "Let's go home before I paint the President's furniture in your sweet cum."

"Tempting," I grin. "But I need to get back to my apartment first. I need my laptop and a few clothes."

He lets go of my chin as the grave expression from earlier returns to his face.

"You can't go back there, angel. Not for a while."

My brows knit together in confusion. "What? Why not?"

I watch his mouth move, the words registering.

My bones shake with fear, and I hold onto him, not knowing how to react.

"Someone broke into your apartment an hour ago. There's blood... everywhere. And one of my men is dead."

"What...?" I stare at him with wide eyes. I bring my hand to my mouth, adrenaline rushing through my veins at the thought of my imminent death.

"Which means that when you saw that orange," he continues, "chances are they were there minutes before you saw it. I'm sorry, Dove, but I'm no longer leaving you out of my sight."

SIXTEEN

I spend the next two weeks at Rowan's house, working extra hours from my laptop so I can compensate for the lack of physical presence at the office.

I hate hiding in here like a scared mouse, but the truth is... I *am* scared. I'm terrified for my life. I'm just a girl from the suburbs who somehow got mixed up with the most hunted man in the country. And now *I'm* the hunted one.

That's why, to my shame, I didn't fight Rowan too much when he asked—no, scratch that—when he *told* me I wouldn't be going to work anymore. But since he had Saint deliver some of my items here, that didn't stop me from putting in the hours online. What else am I supposed to do?

Rowan is always in the house, though he might as well not be here at all. He's always on the phone, or having meetings in his office, or staying up to work until dawn. I feel bad, knowing I'm adding to his already packed schedule.

He's tired. I can see it on his face when he smiles at me. I wish I could do something to help. Anything. But I still don't fully understand what we're up against. And every time I ask him about it, he tells me it's safer for me not to know the details.

So I try to focus on things that *are* in my power—things like making sure he eats. Like making sure he gets enough sleep even when he argues that he's not tired. He never asks me for anything, but I need him to do it. I need him to lean on me as much as I lean on him, or I'll end up feeling like a burden.

I cut up a handful of mushrooms on a wooden board, the sharp knife slicing through them with ease. The knob of butter I threw in the pan is already melting, so I throw them in along with the onion, cherry tomatoes, and garlic I've just diced.

The rich, nutty smell of sizzling vegetables wafts all over me, spreading the sun-kissed aromas from the garden into the room. I then add a teaspoon of tomato puree, along with some fresh herbs and pappardelle pasta, finishing it off with a huge heap of creamy parmesan.

Rowan is still in a meeting right now with someone I've never met before. It's past ten at night and he skipped dinner, so I want to make sure he gets something in his system. Even if I have to bother them from whatever they're talking about.

"Rowan?" I ask, knocking on his office door softer than I indented.

A few seconds pass, and then the door opens fully.

Rowan's tall figure towers above me, hair disheveled and the sleeves of his shirt rolled up to his elbows.

"Sorry to disturb you, I just... it's late. And you didn't come for dinner," I say, pushing the bowl of warm pasta toward him. I move away from the gap created by the door so his guest doesn't see me dressed in nothing but my nightgown.

Dragging a hand down his face, Rowan looks behind him at the man in his office, then back at me. His eyes linger on the curve of my breasts and at the top of my thighs where the nightgown barely covers anything. I'm already squeezing my legs together. Hard.

"Is this a bad time?"

He shakes his head, his eyes hooded as he extends his hand toward me, pulling me in.

"Rowan," I murmur, tingles of arousal creeping into my pussy.

Whatever he's thinking right now can't be good. We haven't had more than a few moments together in days. He's probably as needy as I am.

"Safe word," he demands, pulling me farther into the room inch by inch.

"It's..." I breathe in, eyeing the other man sitting in one of Rowan's armchairs. "Pink."

A deep, approving rumble escapes Rowan's chest as he takes the bowl from my hand and places it on his office desk.

"Say hello to my friend, angel."

I gulp, forcing a smile as I understand exactly what Rowan wants to do.

The man—a solid wall of muscle with years of

austere conditions and habits etched on his features—looks back at me, smirking, his cheek nestled into the cradle of his hand as his elbow supports him on the armrest.

"H-Hello," I whisper.

Behind me, I hear Rowan taking a seat on the adjacent armchair, leaving me to stand in between them like prey. I turn to look at him, a plea in my eyes for him to tell me what to do, so I can stop feeling awkward.

Lifting his chin to meet my gaze, he pats his leg, saying, "Come here."

I hurry into his arms, lowering myself to sit on his lap, fully aware that his friend is watching me.

"You don't want to eat?" I ask as he positions me to face the man instead of cradling him.

Rowan's hands roam freely across my bare legs, dipping under the edges of my nightgown until he reaches the sides of my panties.

"Oh, I'll eat. And so will Leon." He flicks my ear with his tongue, whispering, "Just not the pasta."

Pulling my panties down to the middle of my thighs, my breathing quickens, and I close my eyes in a futile attempt to hide myself from Leon's persistent gaze.

"Say your safe word, angel."

But I surprise myself—and him—when I place my hands on top of his, slowly pulling down my panties until they slide off my legs and onto the floor. I'm naked under the sheer layer of silk barely covering me, and it makes my pussy wet just thinking about it.

I shake my head against his chest.

"That so?" He grunts in my ear, spreading my legs

with his hands and keeping them locked in place with his knees. "In that case..." He pulls my nightgown up, revealing my sleek pussy while I squirm with arousal in his lap. "She's all yours, Leon."

Leon's low chuckle fills the room before he tilts his glass backward, gulping the rest of whatever liquid he had left. He lowers himself to the floor, watching my pussy before he looks up into my nervous eyes. Is he going to touch me? What is he going to do?

I look away, embarrassed, feeling another hand stroking the skin on my inner thigh. And another one. And then Rowan's hands poking under my nightgown, squeezing my bare breasts.

I suck in a breath, my nipples so hard they're practically grazing Rowan's skin, my pussy leaking with arousal into his lap. I'm making a mess on his clothes. Fuck.

Leon's hair brushes against my legs, and I moan from the tickling sensation while I bury my head in the crook of Rowan's neck.

"You're doing so well, angel. Don't move. He's going to make you feel really good. Aren't you, Leon?"

Leon doesn't have to answer with words. Because as soon as his tongue touches my clit, I jolt in Rowan's arms, moaning, legs shaking as the pleasure starts building up. Rowan uses his strength to pin me down to his body, whispering more praise into my ear as Leon licks me where I need it most. Soft. Hard. Slow. Fast. In every way that hits the right places, and in every way that makes my body come alive for the two of them.

This is crazy. I don't know this man. I'm cheating on

my boyfriend right now, and he's letting me. No, he's *indulging* me. How can I—

"Ahhh," I moan when Leon's fingers dip inside my pussy, curling them upward as they reach the depths of my pulsing channel. My legs twitch uncontrollably, but Rowan's knees continue to hold me in place. I am completely at their mercy, with no way to move even if I wanted to.

But I don't want to. God, I really fucking don't.

"Rowan—" I plead, because calling Leon's name would be completely obscene.

"That's my good girl," he murmurs against my skin, sending goose bumps all over my body. "Is he making your pussy come? Do you enjoy having my friend eat you up? Tell me."

"Y-Yes," I squirm harder, shameless in my attempt to rub my pussy against Leon's tongue and getting frustrated when I'm unable to do so. Rowan's grasp on my limbs is so tight I can barely move.

"Yes. Please, Rowan, tell him to—"

Before I get to finish my sentence, bolts of pleasure whip through my flesh with a force that sends me a few inches higher in Rowan's lap. My eyes flutter shut, rolled to the back of my head as I hold onto him while another man is squeezing out every last drop of my arousal with his mouth.

"R-Rowan..." I say, making eye contact with Leon now as he's slowly removing himself from between my legs. His eyes are hooded and his lips are wet, and it makes me blush knowing where they were and how he was maneuvering my body just moments ago.

"So sweet," Leon murmurs, licking his lips. "Addictive, even. I can't help but wonder what it would feel like wrapped around my cock."

My chest heaves with shallow breaths as I look back at Rowan, not knowing what's next. Are they both going to fuck me at the same time? My pussy tingles with excitement at the thought, but my mind... What if this makes Rowan want to fuck other women too?

"Would you like that, angel? To be filled in two holes at once?"

Fuck. I keep quiet, because I know that once I shut it down, I can't change my mind.

I want this. But I can't have it. I can't justify it. It's not fair to Rowan.

"Your silence kind of sounds like a yes, princess," Leon says.

My eyes snap back to his, to his still-wet lips, and to the fingers that are still rubbing me slowly between my legs.

"Pink," I whisper, and Rowan's chest moves behind me with an inhale.

"You know you want it, Dove," Leon presses on, turning my legs to jelly with his gentle strokes.

But then Rowan's knees unlock from between mine, and I let loose a sigh of disappointment when my legs come back together.

"Get out," he tells Leon, his voice so low and grave it slices through the three of us, making my spine straighten up.

"She's clearly entertaining the idea—"

"Get the fuck out. *Now*."

Leon gets up from the floor, straightening his jacket before he shoves a hand in his pocket and walks out of the room. He even throws two fingers in the air in a salute as if he's not bothered in the slightest by Rowan's verbal abuse—but rather annoyed at the interruption. *My* interruption.

I immediately turn in Rowan's arms, facing him with watery eyes.

"Rowan, I'm so, so sorry—"

"Are you all right? Was that too much? I shouldn't have asked you to do this."

"W-What? I... cheated on you just now," I rasp, my voice reduced to almost a whisper as all the ugly feelings come out. "And you're asking me if I'm okay?"

"Cheated on me? How? Was I not here, holding you the entire time?"

"Yes, but, I..."

"You what? Liked it?" He pushes a lock of my hair behind my ear, his lips stretching into a smile. "That was the point, angel. You have nothing to feel guilty about."

"I don't understand. How can you be okay with this? If you did the same thing with another woman, Rowan, I'd..." I shake my head, my eyelashes wet from the first tears spilling out. "It would break me. I wouldn't be able to handle it."

"You're so fucking pretty when you cry," he muses, lost in thought.

I wipe away my stupid tears with the back of my hand, bringing my nightgown back onto my thighs, covering myself up.

"Don't you get it, Dove? I took everything from you. I claimed every single part of your mind... of your body. And still, I want more of you. I'm parched. Starved for whatever else you're willing to give me."

He draws lazy circles around my nipple, waking up every square inch of my body with goose bumps and shivers that race each other down my spine.

"You have the power to bring me to my knees if you wanted to."

With his other hand, he swipes his thumb gently under my eye, taking a tear with it. His tongue darts out when he brings it to his mouth, licking it off.

"You'll be my wife. Carry my children. And live to tell the world stories of how worshipped you were by the madman who claimed you."

His eyes soften on me, and my heart grows with an overwhelming feeling of want—of *need*. Of something so deep and primal that it would terrify me to unleash it all onto him.

"And to answer your question," he continues, "it's about control. About knowing that even when another man licks your pretty pussy while you're squirming in my arms, I'm still the one who has the power to shut it down if I want to. *I* am the one who gives you that pleasure—not Leon, not any other man. Because *I* allow it. Does that make sense?"

I nod, taking in what he's telling me. I wish I could crawl into his head and figure out the way he thinks about the world. I've never met a man like him before, that's for sure.

A few moments of shared silence pass before one of

us speaks again.

"Can I ask you something?" I say.

He sighs, smiling. "You can ask me anything you want. But be prepared for answers you might not want to hear. Or for no answer at all. I'd put you in danger if I told you some of the things you probably want to know."

"I'm already in danger, though, aren't I?"

"Not unless you leave my sight. If the EFW were to get ahold of you, angel..." he frowns, "they'd want to know everything I may have revealed to you about my plans. That won't happen, of course, but I'm not taking any chances."

"Well, this isn't about the EFW. This is about you. And me. I keep getting the feeling that there's something you're not telling me about us. You said you'll tell me what I mean to you one day. What does that mean?"

Rowan drags a hand through his hair, leaning his head back against the armchair. His other hand lowers to the pocket of his slacks, coming out with his phone in it.

"What we have, Dove, is not merely a product of these past few weeks spent together. Not to me, at least."

"Okay," I say, pondering his words, as I watch him scroll through his phone looking for something.

"I'm only showing you this because I believe you now know this is real between us."

I nod, though my anxiety slowly flares up. Show me *what*?

Handing me the phone, I continue to look at him before slowly lowering my gaze to the screen.

"I love you," he says. "And I've had five long years to love you without you knowing it."

Confusion roils around me as every room of my apartment flashes before my eyes.

"After Cole's death, after meeting you that day... I had to make sure you were protected, even if I couldn't physically be there for you. Because the EFW doesn't just want us—they've tried targeting our families in the past. So I knew they'd target you and your parents as well with Cole being gone. Him dying meant there was no one looking over you anymore."

Rowan put *cameras* all over my apartment.

"But the more I watched you... the more I heard you come with my name on your lips night after night, I couldn't help but become completely obsessed with you. Then I started watching you everywhere else. I watched the televised court cases you and your boss won and lost. I watched you shine, and I watched you crumble, and my heart kept asking, *begging* for you.

"For a while, I told myself I had to let you be, because I knew the kind of danger I'd put you in once I reached out. Still, every time I wanted to come and meet you, there was always some obstacle—something major, like a new attack or a new threat that needed my attention. At some point, I even started thinking someone was intentionally keeping me away from you."

My heart leaps to my throat as I look back up from the phone, searching his eyes.

"And then, against my better judgment, I called. Because you put a fucking spell on me, and that day I snapped. I realized there was no going back for me after knowing you. But that isn't even the worst part. You know why, Dove?

"W-Why?"

"Because I'm not sorry for making you mine. Even if I know I fucked up your life by... caging you in our home to protect you from threats you shouldn't even have to worry about."

I look into his eyes, my blood boiling with a feeling I can't yet recognize.

Rage.

Fear.

Lust.

Pure, undiluted obsession.

And a dash of madness, because only a crazy person would find what he did romantic.

"I thought... I thought you were a good man."

His eyes darken, hands dipping back under my nightgown.

"Who told you that?"

SEVENTEEN

They say love makes you do crazy things—things that go against everything you believe in and everything you think you are. Things you'd never fathom you'd be able to carry out. For so long, I refused to believe one's mind could be coerced so easily into committing crimes in the name of love. But falling for Rowan—and being loved so unapologetically—has proved every single one of these claims right.

He watched me. Stalked me. Invaded my privacy in so many moments of my life. If I had any brains in my skull, I'd run far away from this man and go back to what life was before him.

Except... there is no *before* Rowan. There's only the aftermath of him loving me, of me being completely engrossed by his fierce claim over my heart. I couldn't go back to that "before" even if I wanted to. Because the moment he asked me to be his, it's like something shifted in the universe and every other possible door of my destiny slammed shut.

I've called Rowan my monster before, not because

I'm afraid of him, but because I understood from the very beginning the kinds of things he was willing to do—the lengths he'd go to—to get what he wants.

Firing my bodyguard was tame, Cam told me. But stalking someone for years and falling madly in love with her through a bunch of screens? That's pretty crazy. That's pretty fucking insane. And so is turning a blind eye to the fact. So at this point, I don't even know who's crazier between the two of us.

I'm watching the news on the TV upstairs, following Rowan with my eyes on the screen. It's old footage of him visiting the White House and shaking hands with various politicians, despite the news being fresh.

The Coalition occupied two-thirds of the Ridge after recently being pushed back. Political scientists are speculating Austria has a play in this, in helping them. And the question on everyone's lips is, "What will Commander Rowan King do about that"?

"It's not Austria," he says from behind me, startling me.

I turn around, seeing him lean against the doorframe with his arms crossed at his chest, muscles bulging against his black T-shirt.

"The EFW...?" I ponder, lifting myself to a sitting position on the couch.

Rowan nods, and a knot forms in my gut.

"What are you going to do? You can't tell the country about their existence, can you?"

"No. It'd be like telling them aliens are real," he snorts. "I'm going to have to lie. I'm going to have to make allies with people who don't deserve it. Because the alternative..." He walks into the room, dragging a hand through his hair. "The alternative is they win, and the whole fucking world loses instead."

I don't even dare ask him what the hell that means. It's as if he's telling me over and over again that the boogeyman is real. And every time he does, I bring my knees closer to my chest, hiding in my shell.

I turn back to the TV, changing the program to some random movie I don't intend to watch.

"Angel..." he groans, approaching me. His hand caresses the top of my head and I close my eyes, focusing on the feeling of him. He slides it down to my chin, lifting it up so I can look at him. "Talk to me. What's going on in that beautiful mind of yours?"

"Don't ask me that," I say, jerking away from his touch. His nostrils flare, and a sense of pride flashes through me at the fact. "I'm not ready to talk to you about last night."

"Dove—"

Before he can say whatever he wants to say, his eyes slide over to my ringing phone on the glass mini table, the vibrations making it spin slowly in place. I extend my hand forward to pick it up, an unknown number flashing on the screen.

"Can I get some privacy, or is that out of the question now that I'm living in your home?"

"*Our* home," he drawls. "Who's calling?"

I puff out a sigh of frustration, dragging a hand through my hair as I tap to answer the call.

"Hello? Who is this?"

"Dove Finnegan?" a woman asks almost immediately.

A beeping sound in the background muddles her voice, along with a bunch of different conversations happening all at once.

"Yes, it's me," I say, my body frozen in place.

"I'm calling from St. Francis Hospital. Your mother, Clarise Finnegan, was brought here an hour ago after an unfortunate car accident. She's in surgery right now."

My eyes snap to Rowan's, wide in shock.

"Um," I say, swallowing back tears. "How bad... how bad is it?"

There's a short pause. "We're doing everything we can to save her."

I nod frantically, even though she can't see me. "Okay, thank you," I mumble, shutting down the call.

I get up from the couch, moving past Rowan, who follows me around with his eyes.

"Dove?" he calls out from somewhere behind me.

I go into the walk-in closet and choose a random pair of jeans and a T-shirt, trying my hardest not to have a breakdown right now.

"Angel..." he echoes, and I turn to meet his eyes, rage and despair twisting all my features into an almost ugly cry.

"I'm going, Rowan! Don't even *think* to tell me otherwise."

"You know that's not possible," he says.

"I don't care! Besides, I bet you have spies working for you in the hospital anyway." I laugh nervously. "I'm surprised you haven't implanted a GPS tracker in me yet."

His eyes narrow, jaw clenching at the same time.

"It's on the list."

"Oh, is it now?" I shake my head while pulling the jeans up to my hips and buttoning them up. "What about a shock collar too, then, like the fucking President put on his wife? *God*!"

"Keep giving me this attitude, and I'll buy you one today."

I sniff back tears, going into the en-suite bathroom to roughly brush my hair, tugging at the tangled ends until some of them break.

"Come here," he says, following me inside. His hand brushes my shoulder, gently pulling me into his chest.

"*No,*" I cry out. "You don't get to touch me after what you told me last night. You had no right, Rowan. No right to do what you did all those years! Watching over someone is one thing. But stalking me? Watching me in my privacy, following every step I take?"

"Come here, angel. Let me hold you."

He pulls me in, more forcefully this time, and I have no choice but to follow his command.

"I hate you. I hate you so fucking much!" I cry, pounding his chest with my open palms.

He holds my head with one hand and my waist with the other, keeping our bodies close together.

"It'd probably be better for you if you did, but you don't. Not really. You just hate that you love us so much."

"What you did was crazy. Do you at least understand that?"

"I never said it wasn't."

I take a few long breaths, trying to calm down, before I push myself away from him once again. To my surprise, he lets go this time.

"I need to go see my mom," I say, wiping away my tears. "I don't know if she's going to make it."

Even saying those words out loud breaks something in me I'm not sure how to fix.

First, my brother. Now my mom too. This can't happen. She *can't* die on me. I won't accept that.

"Give me half an hour to close down the hospital. Then we can go see her. All right?"

Close down the hospital? Sure, another thing to add to the list of Rowan's obnoxious plans. I don't even question this one. As long as I get to that damned hospital, he can do whatever he wants.

"Fine," I rasp, resuming brushing my hair.

I see his figure in the mirror in front of me—in stark contrast to mine, a sobbing and disheveled mess. He looks calm, collected, and cold as ice. The face of Commander Rowan King, not the face of my lover. As if this is some sort of attack against his own, and he needs to figure out his plans to strike back.

He opens his mouth to say something, but the words never come out. Instead, he takes his phone out of his pocket and starts making calls.

We enter the hospital through the rear atrium, away from the main avenue. No reporters are here, and I wonder if somehow Rowan made it so that no one knows where we are. My entire body tingles from all the stress that courses freely through my aching veins.

Rowan holds my hand as he makes his way through the empty corridors like he knows exactly where we're supposed to go. I let him do it, since I don't have much energy in me to deal with the situation. I just want to see my mom.

We reach the main desk, and the receptionist—a kind-looking, middle-aged woman—immediately notices us. Lines cover her earth-brown skin, as if she spends too many hours on the job.

"Clarise Finnegan," Rowan says, placing a hand on her desk, leaning forward. "What state is she in? When can we see her?"

"I'm sorry, sir, but only family members can—"

"I'm Dove Finnegan, her daughter," I chime in. "Please, can you tell us where she is?"

She looks at me, her lips thinning as she nods.

"She's still in surgery. From what we know, a speeding car hit her as she was crossing the street. She hit her head, causing internal bleeding. One of her lungs got punctured too. She's in a precarious state right now, but the doctors are doing everything they can to help her push through. As soon as she's out and you can see her, I'll let you know."

"It's bad, but... she'll make it, right? She's going to be all right," I say, voice trembling as Rowan slides his arm around my shoulders, bringing me closer to him.

"I'm really sorry," the woman says.

"Who's the doctor in charge of this?" Rowan asks.

"Franco Pierce. I can assure you, sir, he is very good at what he does."

"I know. He's the best in Washington. Keep us posted, please. I want an update every hour with her condition."

"Well, I mean, since you closed the entire hospital down... sure, I can do that." The woman rolls her eyes, then looks down at the scattered papers on her side of the desk.

"Do we have a problem, Miss..." Rowan looks at her name tag, eyes narrowing on her. "Abena?"

"None at all," she says, forcing a smile. "It's just kind of unfair to the other visitors, don't you think? All of you politicians think you can just wave a magic wand and get it your way while the rest of us sit back and let you do as you please, whenever you want."

I can practically feel Rowan's rage simmering underneath his skin. He smiles back at her, but doesn't say anything. He could, though, couldn't he? He could use his power to get her fired, or God knows what else he's thinking of right now.

But I relax a little when I feel his chest release a breath instead.

"I do apologize for the inconvenience. But for reasons I am not at liberty to reveal, this was the only way we could be here with Clarise right now. I hope we can get out of your way as soon as possible and let you get back to saving lives."

Abena nods, looking somewhat satisfied with his answer. But not enough not to give him a side-eye look when we leave her desk and head for the waiting room. I smile apologetically her way before we both disappear by taking the corner.

"Sit down, angel. This could be a while."

I plop down onto a chair, nervous and defeated, propping my elbow on the armrest as I rub my forehead with my hand.

"You don't have to stay. I'm sure you have more important things to do today," I tell him.

"There is nothing in this fucking world more important to me than you. I'm here."

I look up at him, eyebrows furrowed from the nerves still swarming in my gut.

"You haven't even apologized."

"That's because I'm not sorry," he says, very matter-of-fact.

He plops down in the chair next to mine, knees apart and forearms on his thighs. A nurse rushes down the corridor, in the distance, and we both follow her with our eyes.

"Seriously? Then how do you expect me to forgive you?"

"You don't have to forgive me. Hate me or love me, it makes no difference to me. You'll still be mine."

"You're infuriating."

He turns his head to look at me, a faint smile plastered on his lush lips.

Goddamn him. He knows I love him too. I even don't have to say it; it's probably written all over my face right now. I open my mouth to say something, but his phone rings in the pocket of his slacks.

He groans, pulling it out. "What?" he asks.

It doesn't take long before he gets up from his chair, lifting a finger in the air to tell me it'll take a moment. I nod, following him with my eyes until he reaches the end of the corridor and resumes his conversation. I zone out for a few long minutes, looking at nothing in particular, when a pair of white Crocs enters my field of vision.

"Dove Finnegan?" The man's voice startles me.

I lift my gaze to him, noticing he's wearing a white scrubs and a blue shirt underneath. This must be doctor Franco Pierce, the one the receptionist was talking about.

"H-Hello. Yes. How is she?" I ask, getting up and crossing my arms at my chest.

"Stable right now. You can see her for a few moments if you'd like, while we transfer her into her new room."

"Yes, please. Thank you so much. I just need to go tell my—"

"Ah, sorry, if this isn't a good time, I'll come back in a few hours to get you. Like I said, you can only see her for a few moments if you come with me now."

I weigh my options, looking in the distance at Rowan, who is still on the phone. He's rubbing his forehead, annoyed at whatever news the person on the other line gives him.

"No, it's fine, I'll see her now, thank you," I say, getting up to follow him.

If I can only be with my mom for a few moments, I'll probably get back here before Rowan ends his call anyway.

"So... so she's okay?" I ask, hurrying after him. "I thought the surgery was going to take a few hours."

We take the corner into another corridor—a long, dark hallway where no one seems to be working right now.

"Doctor Pierce?" I press on when he doesn't answer.

"Right this way," he says, completely ignoring me.

We take another corner and I stop walking, the hairs on the back of my neck standing up.

For some reason, this doesn't feel right. I shouldn't be alone out here, even if Rowan closed down the hospital. My apartment was just broken into recently, after all.

"I'm sorry, but I think I'll get back to my—"

The rest of my sentence trails off as someone presses a hand to my mouth, grabbing me from behind.

I try to scream, but it comes out muffled, as if I'm under water.

Doctor Pierce sees it—all of it—then continues walking, completely unfazed.

I kick my legs back, thrashing in my captor's arms. A sharp pain erupts on the side of my neck, a needle poking through my skin while foreign liquid enters my bloodstream.

I hear Rowan's voice in the distance, desperate and rough as he calls for me.

I try to call out his name, but my lips are numb.

My eyes roll to the back of my head, and within the

next few seconds, all I see is black.

EIGHTEEN

The first thing I hear is the rattling of chains. Rough, cold, and tight—chains that grip my hands together above my head, digging into my flesh.

My skin buzzes back to life, waking up under the droplets of liquid coating it. A warm liquid. Sticky, and with a metallic smell that wafts through the air around me. It feels like blood, but I don't want to come to that conclusion just yet.

My eyelids feel heavy, and it's too much of an effort to blink. So I rest in the darkness for a while longer, hoping my body will wake itself up from whatever nightmare I'm having right now.

A whimper escapes my lips as I shift, trying to pull my hands back along my torso. The pain gets so strong I have no choice but to cry out, my own echo coming back to hit me like a boomerang.

"Wake up, Dove," a hushed voice tells me. A voice I recognize, but I can't quite match it to anyone I know.

I don't want to, I answer him in my mind.

I must be mumbling unintelligible words, because whoever is with me starts cursing under their breath.

My dry lips smack together, begging for water. And with that realization, a throbbing headache nests in my skull, making me scrunch my already-closed eyes.

"Please..." I mumble, to no one in particular. "I'm so thirsty."

"Dove, listen to me. I don't have much time," the voice says, and I remember, once again, that I can't quite place it. It kind of sounds like... "They're going to ask you questions. Tell them what you know. And then I'll see you in a few days, after your initiation."

"W-Who?" I smack my dry lips again. "Who is this? Please, my wrists hurt."

"Don't fight them. Don't put yourself in danger for nothing. Just tell them what you know. I'll do my best to help you in here before he gets ahold of you."

"Who?" I whimper.

"Rowan. Before Rowan gets ahold of you."

"Where am I?" My chest starts heaving, adrenaline pumping into my veins as my whole body wakes up. "Who are you?!" I open my eyes, webs of fog clouding my vision as I try to register my surroundings.

"They won't rape you. We're all under an oath of celibacy. But they will hurt you, Dove. So don't get clever—just tell them what you know. Promise me," he says, his voice sounding desperate.

I blink rapidly, tears washing my blind spots away. The face of a man I recognize comes into view.

It's so dark in here, but I can see the scar crossing his left eye.

I can see his hair, brown and buzz-cut.

I can see his eyes, colder and more distant than they've ever been.

I see all of it, but I still shake my head, sobbing as the memories come back to life.

"This isn't real. You can't be here," I cry out, not even caring about the pain in my wrists as I tug on the chains.

But it is real. And he is here.

My dead brother, Cole, is very much still alive.

END OF BOOK 1

Thank you for taking the time to read ***Under His Command***.

I know the first book ended on a huge cliffhanger. So before the second book comes around, I'd like to offer you a BONUS CHAPTER available at rheaharp.com when you sign up for my newsletter. This chapter is told from Rowan's perspective, and I think you're going to love it!

Here are just a few reactions I received about it:

"Fucking loved the chapter! Waiting for Book 2 eagerly!!!!!!!!!!!!!" – Chaitali
"Girl you ate up with this chapter!!!!!!!!!!" - Matthania
"I loveeee it can't wait for it to continue" – Natalia
"Here I thought nothing would make me as eager to read the next chapter as the last one but boy was I wrong! – Alexia
"Oh my God, I really loved that. Thank you for that chapter." - Daniela

Whether you get the bonus chapter or not, I'd be eternally grateful if you could leave a review on this book before moving on. Thank you so very much for reading!

ACKNOWLEDGEMENTS

My partner has been my rock throughout this entire author journey. There were (and still are) many moments when I didn't believe in myself, but he always does. Thank you. I love you so much it hurts.

I would also like to thank all my online readers for waking me up to tons of excited comments and reactions to this story every single morning. It's the most amazing feeling an author can have, and I'm eternally grateful for your support.

Last but not least, I'd like to extend my gratitude to my editor, Christina, my cover artist, Avery, and everyone on DD who has helped me shape this story into what it is today. I truly couldn't have done it without you! Thank you!

ABOUT THE AUTHOR

Rhea Harp is a dark romance writer based in the heart of Transylvania. She loves to enjoy a glass of dry wine during her writing sessions. And she's often found listening to the melancholic songs of The Weeknd. When she's not writing, she's trying out new recipes or playing board games with her partner and friends.

To contact Rhea, sign up for her newsletter at rheaharp.com. She reads every single email and replies to as many as she can. Plus, by signing up, you also get access to exclusive content and news about upcoming book releases.

If you would like to join Rhea's ARC team or street team for her upcoming books, please send an email to rhea@rheaharp.com saying "ARC" or "STREET" (or both), and she will send you more information.

Alternatively, follow Rhea Harp on Instagram: @rheaharpauthor

Made in United States
North Haven, CT
27 March 2025

67289139R00111